George Lorimer

Leaves From the Buik of the West Kirke

George Lorimer

Leaves From the Buik of the West Kirke

ISBN/EAN: 9783337049133

Printed in Europe, USA, Canada, Australia, Japan

Cover: Foto ©Andreas Hilbeck / pixelio.de

More available books at **www.hansebooks.com**

LEAVES FROM

The Buik of the West Kirke

BY

GEORGE LORIMER

WITH A PREFACE BY THE

REV. JAMES MACGREGOR, D.D.
SENIOR MINISTER OF ST. CUTHBERT'S

EDINBURGH: DAVID DOUGLAS

1885

PRINTED BY T. AND A. CONSTABLE, PRINTERS TO HER MAJESTY.
AT THE EDINBURGH UNIVERSITY PRESS.

PREFACE.

IN bringing the present collection of papers under the notice of the Congregation, a word of explanation is necessary, first, as to the title under which they make their appearance, and, second, as to their appearance at all.

In the course of two hundred years there had accumulated in the repositories of the Kirk-Session of St. Cuthbert's a large and heterogeneous mass of written material, which it was thought of importance to weed out and arrange. This heavy but congenial task was assigned to our Elder, Mr. George Lorimer. Although it was to him a labour of love, few can have any adequate idea of the time and patience which were expended in the study and arrangement of these old documents.

The most noteworthy of them have been put together, and now form a goodly folio of some 400 pages, to which the appropriate title has been given of 'The Buik of the West Kirke.'

To students, alike of Church History and of our 'Domestic Annals,' it contains much that is interesting.

As Mr. Lorimer, from previous studies, was well informed regarding the period covered by these documents, he was induced to give a Lecture on the subject to our young men. As that

Lecture seemed to me well worthy of a wider audience than that to which it was originally addressed, he kindly consented, at my request, to publish it in its present form. As the bulk of the matter, and all, save one, of the illustrations in the present volume have been taken from the 'Buik of the West Kirke,' it seemed not inappropriate to borrow its name. For the illustrations, which so greatly add to its attractions, we are indebted to the 'camera' of another member of our Kirk-Session, Mr. George A. Panton, to whom our grateful acknowledgments are due.

The sketches which follow refer mainly to the last twenty years of the seventeenth century, a period of our Church History second to none in interest and importance. It was a period which, though short, saw the worst days of the persecution of the Covenanters—'the killing-time,' as it was called—and the quiet years which followed the passing of the Revolution Settlement.

In this little volume there will be found much that is interesting with regard to the manners and customs of our forefathers, and especially of those who, like ourselves, were parishioners of St. Cuthbert's and members of the West Kirk. It is hoped that, on this account, it may prove acceptable to the members of the present Congregation.

JAMES MACGREGOR.

11 CUMIN PLACE, GRANGE,
    EDINBURGH, *9th Nov.* 1885.

CONTENTS.

CHAPTER VI.

CHAPTER VII.

CHAPTER VIII.

ILLUSTRATIONS.

CHAPTER I.

In his interesting *History of the West Church*, the late Mr. Sime, who was for a long time its Recorder, has presented to us a narrative of the fortunes of the edifice; of the events most noteworthy in the incumbency of the various pastors; and in placing before us more than one interesting picture of the customs of bygone times, has served to illustrate in a very striking manner the truth of the well-worn proverb, *Tempora mutantur nos et mutamur in illis.* In the scanty space which he has allowed himself, however, it was impossible to do full justice to the merits of his theme. The narrative of events occurring throughout a period of three hundred years cannot without prejudice be compressed within the boards of a tiny duodecimo; and, considering his special qualifications for the work, it is a matter for regret that he did not allow himself a little more scope. He probably feared that the circle to which he had to appeal was but a limited one, and planned his work accordingly. Perhaps he was right, and one thing is pretty certain, that the History, as a whole, will never be rewritten. All that is proposed in the present volume is to examine a little more carefully the last twenty years of the seventeenth century, and with the aid of the Church's own records, and other means available, to make ourselves a little more familiar

A

with matters ecclesiastical at the time in general, and with those
of the West Church in particular.

The old Church of St. Cuthbert, although occupying a
central position in the parish, was yet in a comparatively lonely
situation, with but few dwelling-houses of any sort in its vicinity;
and we may picture it to ourselves as a quaint old-fashioned
edifice, standing on the marshy shore of the Nor' Loch, the very
picture, but for the overshadowing ramparts of the Castle, of a
quiet country parish church. According to Gordon of Rothiemay,
whose well-known view of Edinburgh was executed in 1647, it
was a long narrow building, with one transept or aisle on the
south, a high square tower of three stories at the south-west
corner, and a belfry. But, between then and 1680, the beginning
of the period with which we have to do, and again before its
close, it suffered severely from the batteries of the Castle, first
during its siege by Oliver Cromwell, and again when it was held
by the Duke of Gordon for King James at the time of the
Revolution ; and by the year 1700 its various renovations had
made it a building as unlike that portrayed by Gordon as
could well be—curious, and it must· be admitted hideous, in the
extreme, if it was at all like the print of it given in Sime's
History. According to it, it seems to have consisted of several
mean houses squeezed together, and, but for its belfry tower,
might have been taken for a collection of granaries, or indeed
almost anything rather than an ecclesiastical edifice. Above it
frowned the battlements of the Castle, but of the adjacent city
nothing was visible, save possibly the outline of the houses in
the Lawnmarket.

To the north stretched a bleak common, the site of the
present New Town, long possessed by the family of Hepburn of
Bearford, and hence known as Bearford's Parks. Where Princes
Street now stands ran a straight country road, called the Lang

Dykes, by which the dwellers in the eastern end of the parish, Ninian's Row, the modern Greenside, and Broughton, found their way to church, while on the west was one which, issuing from the West Port, led past the church to the Kirkbraehead, and eventually to Stirling.

The outward aspect of the church was singular, but its interior must have been even more so. Formed after no plan, it possessed a number of little galleries stuck up, one above another, to the very rafters. These belonged to the principal heritors and the incorporated trades of the parish, which were comparatively numerous; the Cordiners, or Shoemakers of Portsburgh, of Potterrow, and of Dean, the Hammermen of the West Port, the Wrights and Baxters of Portsburgh, the Tailors of Potterrow, the Millers and Salters of the Water of Leith, are all referred to in the Church records as having their individual lofts or galleries. What would now be called the body of the church was only partially occupied with fixed seats. Here the poorer worshippers brought their stools, or stood. In a prominent place, probably in the north aisle, rose the pillar at the foot of which were stationed offenders against Church discipline, while, nearer to the pulpit, was the standard on which stood the sand-glass, an institution the existence of which would seem at first sight to indicate that our forefathers, no more than ourselves, were fond of long sermons.

Adjoining the church stood the bare walls of what was known as the 'Little Kirk,' erected in 1593, in the palmy days of the pastorate of the great Robert Pont, by far the most eminent of the numerous able men who have filled the pulpit of the West Church. To him belongs the proud distinction of being the only minister of the Reformed Church of Scotland who ever occupied a seat as one of the Judges of the Court of Session, and that at a time when occupying one of its most important

charges. The fame of his learning attracted such crowds of
worshippers, that it was found necessary to provide accommoda-
tion for them, by the erection of an additional place of worship,
a long narrow edifice, stretching westward from the belfry
tower of the main church. It was now a ruin. It had suffered
terribly in the struggle between Cromwell and the defenders of
the Castle, after the battle of Dunbar, and was never afterwards
thoroughly repaired. Indeed by this time it had become a place
of sepulture, and only served to enhance the dreary appearance
of the main church.

The West Church then formed the only place of worship for
a parish whose bounds were far more ample than they are at the
present day. This will be at once apparent by a reference to the
valuation roll of the parish for 1699.[1] It was divided into
numerous districts, to each of which were assigned an elder and
deacon, whose duty it was to take a very particular supervision
of those residing within their bounds. These districts almost
completely surrounded Edinburgh, stretching as they did from
Ninian's Row, along the banks of the Nor' Loch, to the church,
and thence by the West Port and Potterrow to the Pleasance.
This was merely the inner circle; among the more outlying
districts were Pilrig, Craigleith, Saughton, Drumsheugh, then
called Meldrum's Heugh, Braid houses, and Newington.

When, after the Revolution, the Presbyterian party re-
gained possession, the fabric of even the main church was found
to be in a condition so ruinous as to be quite unfit for use as a
place of worship. It had suffered terribly from the fire of the
Duke of Gordon's cannon, which was rather shabby behaviour
on the part of his Grace, as, according to current report, he
profited not a little in his defence of the Castle by the intelligence
which Mr. Guild, St. Cuthbert's last Episcopal minister, was able

[1] See Appendix A.

Bill of affairs

Bought for and giues

for and boy of ...giues

and Loig of Mathous — 18 00

for ... pair of shous — 18 00

for ... pair of shous — 02 00

for and ... giues Siffose — 10 00

for and pound of ... — 05 00

1h euro ... — 04 00

... Loig of ... — 07 00

for ... 3 ... — 06 00

for ... ... — 01 00

for to baco & ... — 10 00

15 : 0 9 00

3 : ... : ..

... . 0 9 . ..

to give him. This feat on the part of the latter, it may be mentioned in passing, cost him dear. It was afterwards given by
the Privy Council as one, along with other reasons, for depriving
him of his charge. It was obviously not the part of the heritors
to repair damages sustained in this way. The Kirk-Session,
therefore, sought the assistance of the Privy Council, and to
propitiate its favour, gave a dinner to those of its number who
had been appointed to examine the damage done. The dinner
bill, which is still in existence, is rather a curiosity, and worthy of
inspection. It being so clearly the interest of the Kirk-Session
to treat their guests well, it may be reasonably assumed that the
dinner would be, for the time, one of the best procurable. It will
be noticed that there is neither soup nor fish, but an abundance
of meats of various kinds, and dessert in the shape of figs, raisins,
and biscuits. It suggests what would be thought a very heavy
dinner at the present day, but, from the comparatively moderate
supply of liquor charged for, in a day when hard drinking was
the rule among the upper classes, very likely it was only intended
for luncheon. To be sure the Scotch pynt was equal to three
of our quart bottles, but, even keeping that in view, the amount
of wine used is much smaller than might have been looked for,
as a proportionate concomitant to all the beef and mutton, and
veal and pork and poultry, which went along with it.

The dinner was not without its effect; the damage was
promptly repaired, but, after all was done, it is probable that
the church remained in rather a crazy condition. This would
appear from a curious story told by Wodrow. 'This night,'[1]
he says, 'Glanderston told me that it was reported for a truth at
Borrowstoness that Mr. David Williamson was preaching in his
own church about six weeks since, and in the middle of the
sermon a ratton came, and sat down on his Bible. This made

---

[1] 27th February 1702.

him stop, and after a little pause he told the congregation that this was a message of God to him, and broke off his sermon, and took a formal farewell of his people, and went home, and continues sick.'

Sheriff Napier, in his *Memorials of Dundee*, roguishly suggests that the message, intrusted to such an envoy, must have had some other than a celestial origin. Be that as it may, it seems clear, that the temerity displayed by the individual rat is only to be explained by the assumption that the church was completely overrun by his species, and that, in all probability, he was quite as much at home in the pulpit as Mr. Williamson.

CHAPTER II.

DAVID WILLIAMSON.

DURING the period under consideration the ministers of the West Church were seven in number, four of these being Episcopal, Messrs. Sutherland, Kay, Hepburn, and Guild, and three Presbyterian, Messrs. Williamson, Anderson, and Paterson.

Save one, none of these call for special remark, but, it may be said in passing, of those first mentioned, that there is no reason to believe that they were of the mean and illiterate class to which the curates, who were then generally intruded into Presbyterian pulpits, were said to belong. Hepburn, to whom perhaps most exception may be taken, died at the time of the Revolution. Of those who survived, Kay and Guild lost their churches, practically because they refused to conform to the new order of things, a fact certainly not to their discredit. Sutherland and Guild came from the North, Hepburn from England. The odium of being perverts to an alien form of religion cannot therefore be attributed to them, and it was no more blameworthy in Guild, that he sought to give assistance to King James, then a fugitive, by supplying the Duke of Gordon with information, than it afterwards was in stout-hearted old Neil M'Vicar, when, after Prestonpans, he prayed publicly for King George in defiance of the Pretender's commands. Of David Williamson, however, a good deal may be said. He was a prominent man in his day and generation, and noteworthy in many ways.

The son of a respectable glover of St. Andrews, where he studied, graduating in 1655, he was licensed to preach in 1658, and became minister of the West Church in 1661. In the following year was passed the celebrated Act requiring conformity to the Episcopal *régime*, then instituted, which led to the resignation of their charges by no fewer than three hundred and fifty ministers, but, although he refused to conform, no steps were taken against him, and he continued to officiate until April 1665. Hitherto he had maintained a discreet silence, but his colleague, Mr. Gordon, having preached in favour of the innovations in worship which had been introduced, he replied to him from the pulpit, and boldly attacked the Episcopal ceremonies which his colleague had defended. This led to a complaint, on the part of the latter, to the Court of High Commission, in consequence of which he was 'discharged' to preach at the West Kirk. It was an age when the spirit of prophecy was shed abroad, according to the traditions which have come down to us, and it was quite in keeping with this, that Mr. Williamson, when preaching his farewell sermon, should prophesy his return. His text was, 'Many are called, but few are chosen,' and, at the conclusion of his sermon, he expressed himself thus : 'I still own my relation to this kirk, and am forced from it, but I will return again, and will die minister of this kirk.' The records of the church are now silent on the subject, but that the event was noticed, and that in a way unsatisfactory to one side or other, seems evident from the fact, that the page of the Minute-book, in which the matter would naturally be referred to, has been torn out.

After this he became very obnoxious to the Government, and, in a long list of Covenanters, who were denounced as outlaws, and had to flee for their lives, proclaimed at the market crosses of the principal towns of Scotland, his name stands the very first, although it included those of Donald Cargill, John Welch, and Fraser of Brea. For many years thereafter he lived in comparative seclusion, preaching, as occasion offered, at the risk of his life. His narrow escapes were numerous. Several of these are narrated by Wodrow, who had them from his son John Williamson, minister of Inveresk. On one occasion, he tells us, getting word that his retreat had been discovered, 'he takes his horse, which was a very good one, and free from all pratts (tricks), very early in the morning, and, after he had ridden some miles, his horse takes a stand, and will not go forward. He lighted to see if anything scared him, but observed nothing ; he offered to lead him, but he would go no farther ; whip and spur would not prevail. After he had commended himself to God in prayer, he mounted, and laid the bridle upon its neck, and left himself to Providence : the horse turned about and went pleasantly back to the house whence he came, and, when he came thither, he found that they had been there, and were gone again, so that he could be nowhere so safe.' This was not the only occasion upon which the mysterious instinct of his horse saved him, for, a little later on, riding in haste when the pursuit was hot against him, he came to a point at which the road forked, and knew not which of the ways to take ; 'he stood a little, and commended himself to God's guiding, and the horse went into one of them which led about a little hill, and when he was ridden a little he perceived a party of soldiers upon the other side, and he just missed them by the intervening of the hill, for the roads met beyond the hill, and that very party were seeking him.' 'Thus,' adds Wodrow piously, 'He gives his angels charge over his own, yea he makes for them a covenant with the beasts of the field.' His most

B

notable escape by far was that in which he owed his life
to the assistance of Mrs. Murray of Cherrytrees and her
daughter, the latter of whom he subsequently married ; but its
main outline is probably sufficiently well known, to render any
further allusion to it unnecessary.

While Williamson had thus given signal proof of his
adherence to the cause of the Covenant, he did not share in the
extreme political views latterly put forward by the supporters
of Cameron and Renwick.   He accordingly accepted the
protection offered by the Indulgence of 1687, and returned to
Edinburgh, where he soon gathered together a considerable
congregation, preaching to them at a meeting-house erected at
the Water of Leith, not far from his old church.   Here he continued to labour for a short time ; but the days of Episcopacy
were now numbered : with the successful accomplishment of the
Revolution, it became a thing of the past, and his prophecy, of
twenty-eight years previous, was at last fulfilled.   He returned
to his old church, where he continued to minister until his
death, in 1706.   That he did return to his former charge was
not however to be looked upon as a mere matter of course, and
Wodrow tells us that, the night before the Assembly was to
determine the matter, ' he was in prayer and wrestling all
night, and had many fears and much sorrow, but at length
he got out of them, and when the elders came to him, he
comforted them, and said, " There is no fear."'

Of his eloquence as a preacher there seems sufficient proof in
the fact that he declined calls both to Edinburgh and Glasgow ;
and in that singular volume, the *Memoirs of the Spiritual
Exercises of Elizabeth West*, the authoress, more than once,
speaks of the benefit she derived from his sermons.

Contemporaneous notices are however much more copious
on another point.   Williamson's experiences were of the most

diverse nature. We see him, in the pages of Wodrow, a lonely hunted wanderer, glad of the shelter of a fail dyke behind which to lie down and rest himself amid the snow ; at another time, the chosen of his church, to present its congratulations, at the court of William and Mary, upon their accession to the throne ; but in no particular field was his experience so ample as in that pertaining to matters matrimonial. His was not a patriarchal age ; hence it is somewhat startling to learn that he was married no fewer than seven times. His first wife, Isobel Lindsay, died, leaving an only child, when he was thirty-one years of age. He then married Margaret Scott, and, again a widower, there occurred the romantic episode before alluded to, which led to his marriage with the daughter of Murray of Cherrytrees. The name of his fourth wife, who died in 1692, was Margaret Melwing. It is narrated that his alliances, up to this point, had made him, when in London, an object of interest to Queen Mary's maids of honour; but how much would that interest have been intensified had they known that yet another, and another, and another bride was he to lead to the altar! These three marriages he consummated in three successive years. But if the married bliss enjoyed by Mesdames Williamson Nos. Five and Six was short-lived, it was otherwise with Jean Straiton, the seventh, and she survived to mourn him.

It may be asked, How did he acquire the sobriquet of 'Dainty'? and to that no certain reply can be given, but that he was well known by it during his lifetime is certain. This is shown by a story told of him by Wodrow, amusing, in one sense, although certainly not in another. It appears that shortly before the Revolution, he was preaching at Aberdeen, then the great stronghold of Episcopacy, and, as may be imagined, the advent of one so well known as a Covenanter was not relished. What follows may be given in Wodrow's own words : ' On

Sabbath, when going to preach, they hounded out a poor profane man to meet him on the public street, and sing and dance before him : whether he had a fiddle playing also, I do not mind, but the tune he sang, in dancing before him, was " Dainty Davy. " Mr. Williamson was grieved at the profanation of the Sabbath, and said to somebody with him, " Alas for that poor man! he is now rejecting the last offer he is ever to have of Christ ;" the wretch came not to church, and, that night, died suddenly in a few minutes.'

It is probable that he was by habit dainty, not merely in his tastes but also in his person. It is recorded of him that he was the first clergyman in Scotland who carried a watch, and it is a fact, which no one will venture to deny, that he was eminently a ladies' man. As showing that he was somewhat of an epicure quite an interesting discovery was made recently, by the present writer, in the examination of a vast mass of old vouchers, etc., which, for the last century, have been accumulating in the belfry of the West Church. Amongst these was found a receipt for nothing less than a dish of Christmas mince pies, furnished to the Kirk-Session of the West Church, in December 1690, when Williamson was in sole charge, and must therefore be held responsible for the occurrence. To understand the magnitude of his transgression, looked at from the then prevailing point of view, it must be remembered, that, of old, mince pies were held to possess a deep religious significance, and were eaten in commemoration of that event to which the festival of Christmas owes its origin. Even the learned Selden has not thought them beneath his notice, and gives rules as to their shape, etc., and, to this day, in some parts of England, it is considered unlucky to refuse the first offer of mince pies at Christmas-time. In the eyes of the stern Presbyterians of Covenanting times, they were looked upon with abhorrence as suggestive of Prelacy, to say the least, and their use strictly forbidden.[1] The receipt is to this effect :—' I Christian Kinnimont relict of the umquhile Thomas Fleck, Baxter, and Burgess of Edinburgh, grants me to have received, from Mr. James Hunter of Muirhouse, a crown, and that in full, and compleat payment, of a dish of mincht peys, furnisht be me to him, and discharges him of the samyn, as witness my hand, at Edr., the 29 day of December 1690 years.'

Observe the amount paid—one crown, that is to say, £3 Scots! A leg of mutton, as appears from the bill for the dinner given the same year to the Privy Council, then cost about 12s. Scots, and here we have the equivalent of five legs of mutton lavished upon one dish of mince pies. Now there is nothing costly about a mince pie ;—its ingredients are simple,—even yet a crown would probably furnish quite as many mince pies as the present Kirk-Session of St. Cuthbert's would care to eat, and the extravagant price paid for them to Widow Fleck can only be accounted for by the supposition, that, in baking them at all, she was running, as she knew, a very considerable risk ; the West Kirk Session could certainly not find fault with her, but, in all probability, she lived in Edinburgh, and was under a different jurisdiction. There is something very funny in the spectacle of an ex-Covenanter, one accustomed to all manner of hardships, leading his elders upon forbidden ground in this way : well might he be called Dainty Davy, but we like him none the worse for it.

Latterly, owing to his numerous alliances, he possessed considerable means, which he was not slow to make use of for the benefit of others, and, in January 1700, he generously made over to the Kirk-Session a house, with ground adjoining, now

[1] 9th January 1654. 'Jhonne Keannie, baxter, was this day sharpely rebuked before the Session be the Moderator, for careing pyes on Yooldey. He promised neevir to baike pyes for Yuilday, nor to carie anie that day throwe the streates in tyme comeing, with certificatioune,' etc.—*Records of the Kirk-Session of Aberdeen*, 121.

forming part of the present churchyard, which he had purchased for the purpose of being used as a manse by the junior minister.

Almost the last glimpse we get of him is in 1703, on the occasion when the General Assembly, proving less docile, on the subject of toleration to Episcopacy, than was agreeable in high quarters, was abruptly dissolved by the Lord High Commissioner, the Earl of Seafield. Pensive and melancholy he came out, and when, in company of several others, he was questioned as to his demeanour, he replied, ' That man has raised a flame in the house of God this day, and I am much mistaken if God shortly raise not a flame in his house which noe hand shall quench.' As in other instances, he proved a true prophet, for within a fortnight the luxurious residence which Seafield had but just then newly furnished, was with his library burned to the ground. Seafield was hated for his behaviour in connection with the Darien scheme, and, as he went about crying for help, which almost none would give, he was told he had better fetch water from Barbadoes, and other places, where water had been refused to the Scotch adventurers.

On the 6th August 1706, in a ripe old age, David Williamson was at last gathered to his fathers. The circumstances of his death are related in some detail by his son, the minister of Inveresk, in one of his letters to Wodrow, from which we learn that he died without a word of regret, a sincere and humble Christian. To the Lord Advocate, Sir James Stewart, who spoke to him of the good he had been privileged to do, he replied that he blessed God who gave him a willing mind, but he desired to lean only on the righteousness of Christ.

Three days later his remains were laid to rest beneath the shadow of the church he had loved so much, amid the universal sorrow of his people.

Peace be to his memory !

CHAPTER III.

THE nature of the Church Services conducted in the old West Church at this time is a subject which naturally calls for inquiry, but, at the very outset, a difficulty presents itself in this, that during the earlier half of our period the services were nominally Episcopal, during the latter half they were actually Presbyterian. This initial difficulty is however one more apparent than real. Strange as it may seem, considering the sufferings which thousands underwent, in order to mark their detestation of the system, between Episcopacy, as practised in Lowland Scotland from 1665 to 1689, and the Presbyterianism which followed it, there was, saving the existence of Bishops practically no difference.

In the West Church, at any rate, so far as can be ascertained the only distinction between the earlier and later portion of the period now under review, was, that the church during the second was better filled than during the first. After the return of David Williamson, and the reopening of the church, we can imagine that non-attendance at church, although an offence occasionally referred to at meetings of the Kirk-Session, as an aggravation of others more serious, would be of rare occurrence, —rare to an extent hardly conceivable now-a-days. This arose, not merely from the fact, that the offender, in absenting himself without cause, set all decorum at defiance, but because, within the walls of the church of a Sunday, there were probably more matters of human interest taking place than had occurred elsewhere on any single day of the week previous.

By an edict of Bishop Paterson's, in 1687, it was enacted that marriages should only be celebrated on Sundays, in church, during time of Divine Service. The Bishop was a capital man of business, as can be seen from the rules laid down by him at the only meeting of Session which he ever attended, that of 18th December 1679, and, in issuing this edict, he probably had an eye to the benefit likely to result to the poor, there being always a collection made on such occasions. The rule was relaxed after 1689, but, as it was found that this was to the detriment of the poor, the Kirk-Session resolved, on 8th June 1693, that, for the privilege of not being married in church, the sum of £4 should be paid, as a kind of equivalent for the loss which the poor's stock must thereby incur. It may be therefore safely assumed that the bulk of the marriages would take place in church. Only those who wished to be very fashionable would be married in private.

It was the custom then, as it is now, that Baptism should be administered in public, and that offenders should be publicly rebuked. In a congregation of such importance, marriages and baptisms would be of very common occurrence, while, as for offenders against discipline, their total absence from the place of public repentance would be an event of as rare occurrence as was that of the closing of the gates of the Temple of Janus in the days of Ancient Rome.

Half an hour or thereby before the minister took his place in the pulpit, the reader appeared at his desk, and read such chapters from the Bible as the minister had appointed. As soon as the latter had taken his place, the reading was discontinued, and a Psalm given out by the reader, which he continued to sing with the people, until signalled by the minister to stop, the Psalm being given out line by line for the benefit of those who had no Psalm-books or could not read. The duties of the officiating clergyman then began. During Episcopal times ministers wore cassocks and gowns in the pulpit, but after the Revolution the practice was for them to dress in much the same way as the congregation, and this practice was continued for a considerable time. Even as late as 1709, Dr. Calamy, in the course of a visit to Scotland, records his surprise at the fact that the ministers preached 'in neckcloths and coloured cloaks.'

The minister began by a prayer, in which confession was made, and the holiness and majesty of the Almighty magnified. The sermon followed, after which there was an intercessory prayer for all men, the Church, the Royal Family, subordinate magistrates, and for the sick of the congregation by name ; the Lord's Prayer followed, then a Psalm, and then the benediction.[1] The collection for the poor was taken in little porches erected for the purpose at the entrance to the churchyard. At one time it was made during the service in some churches, but this practice was forbidden by the General Assembly of 1648.

In describing at the outset the appearance of the church, allusion was made to the existence of a standard, in the vicinity of the pulpit, on which was placed a sand-glass. That this was intended to regulate to some extent the length of the sermon seems clear, but that it was placed there in the interests of the congregation only, is very much to be doubted, from the notices, comparatively few and obscure, which have come down to us. It was an age when the staying powers of the preacher were extraordinary, the capacity for the assimilation of doctrinal food on the part of

[1] This description of the method of worship is taken principally from Morer's *Short Account of Scotland.*

his hearers unbounded ; and it would be hard to say whether England or Scotland bore away the palm in this respect, though probably it was the latter. Poor Spalding, in 1642, in one of his frequent grumbles against the innovations of the Rev. Andrew Cant, speaks of the sermons as 'having four hours' doctrine to ilk sermon,' while Principal Baillie, about the same time, in one of his letters about the Westminster Assembly, gives the following account of a conference then held : ' Mr. Marshall prayed at large two hours most divinely, confessing the sins of the members of Assembly. After, Mr. Arrowsmith preached an hour, then a psalm ; thereafter Mr. Vines prayed near two hours, and Mr. Palmer preached an hour, and Mr. Seaman prayed near two hours, then a psalm, after which Mr. Henderson brought them to a sweet conference of the heat confessed in the Assembly.' ' Praying at large' is a very happy expression applied to prayers of such a length. That there should be three examples in the course of one meeting proves the existence of the practice of praying at large ; and the existence of such a practice, in itself, goes far to explain the national rebound in an opposite direction, which took place not long after. These performances, startling as they appear, are however completely eclipsed by one referred to by Wodrow. On this occasion the sermon lasted seven hours. It was inferred that the preacher, the minister of Kinellan, was not quite in his sound mind, but, sane or otherwise, the fact is significant,—no one surely would be so insane as to preach so long to empty pews. That people were willing to sit so long seems clear proof that the duration of the sermon was by no means abnormal.

It may be asked, Of what use was the existence of the glass, if so little respect was paid to it ? If it ran for seven hours, or even four, it might just as well not have been there ; but the fact is, that the length of the service was so entirely within the discretion of the preacher, that he might even direct that the glass be not turned at all. This is seen by a letter from Mr. Williamson of Inveresk, which is quoted by Wodrow. Such a proceeding would doubtless be a little uncommon, a liberty to be resented if frequently indulged in, still it shows how completely the congregation was at the mercy of the minister.

The glass was however useful in another way. Mr. Edgar, in his chapter on ' Public Worship in Olden Times,'[1] has drawn attention to the fact that preachers at this time found difficulty in doing justice to the merits of their text within the compass of one sermon, or rather that the discourse founded on the text occupied more than one Sunday in its delivery. He gives more than one extraordinary example of this, showing that the exposition of a single verse might occupy a couple of months. This practice may be inferred from the account of the presbyterial visitation of the West Church, occurring on page 58, where it is stated that the minister preached on his 'ordinary text.' In such cases the use of the sand-glass is apparent. The sermon always underwent amplification in delivery, according to the frame of the preacher. The subdivisions of the subject were endless, and appropriate halting-places were not so well defined as would be the case now ; hence the flight of time served, as well as anything else, to indicate to the preacher when he should close. The custom had its advantages, doubtless, in the case of spiritual epicures like Elizabeth West, from whose memoirs the existence of the practice can be plainly seen ; but it had also its drawbacks, and, on the whole, it will be generally felt that it would not be desirable to revive it.

So much has been said in the foregoing pages on the subject

---

[1] Those who would seek a thorough acquaintance with Church matters at this time should consult the interesting volume recently published by the Rev. Mr. Edgar of Mauchline, *Old Church Life in Scotland.*

of long sermons, that it is perhaps worth while to give an example
of the way in which the framework was built up, the more so as
there is a very good one ready to hand, found along with other
papers already referred to in the belfry of the church. It is in
the handwriting of Mr. Dunning, Session-Clerk of the West
Church more than a hundred and fifty years ago. It has been
assumed, although probably on insufficient evidence, to have been
delivered by Mr. Pitcairn, who was minister of the West Church
when Whitfield preached in it on the occasion of his first visit
to Scotland.

' *Therefore whosoever heareth these sayings of mine, and doeth them,
I shall liken him to a wise man, that built his house upon a
rock.'*—MAT. vii. 24.

From w⁰ 2 Quest. may be started by us. 1. What have
we done with all Christ's sayings we have heard. 2. How are
we fitted for what stress of Weather may overtake us : here we
have two duties commended. 1. Hearing, 2. Doing—the ad-
vantageousness of hearing and doing. 2. Disadvantageousness
or loss in hearing & not doing from which Observe that as
Christ will have us to hear so he teaches us to improve qᵗ we
hear and that, by Alarms on the one hand, and Instructions on
the other—from the words there are six Alarms.

ALARM 1. That people may live all their days under a preaching ministry, and Chr., and yᵗ never ken one
another.

ALARM 2. That a person may get a Delusion under Preaching
that may go to Eternity wᵗ them and no less
than Eternal rejection can convince them of it.

ALARM 3. There is a Stress of Weather awaiting all, and none
but such as hear & improve Chr. Saying or
Preaching will stand it out.

ALARM 4. That folk may be at mickle work building a house and, after all, lose both their pains and profit because they build not on a Rock.

ALARM 5. That folk may have their Light and Profession bettered by preaching, yet both it and they may be cast over ye barrd at last.

ALARM 6. That this is not the case of a few but of many which should make us get to our [*word missing*] that we be not found asleep like Jonah in the storm.

INSTRUCTION 1. When Preaching is done our Work is to begin, he is a right hearer who, the nearer the Sabbath is to ending, has his work the thronger, and so divides the week as to improve in the one half, & prepares for the next Sabbath by the other half.

INSTRUCTION 2. When Preaching is improven for bringing us the nearer Christ in conformity.

INSTRUCTION 3. When it fits & prepares us for Stress of Weather.

INSTRUCTION 4. When it tends to build a house for Christ in our hearts by some stones laid on ye wall or some pinnings put in the wall.

INSTRUCTION 5. When our Walk and Practice shines more by our hearing.

INSTRUCTION 6. When we are thereby improven more and fitted for Judgement wherefore doth Christ take so much pains upon us.

REASON 1. Because otherwise by not improving, all his pains and labour would be lost.

REASON 2. Because he is so serious in the Matters of our Salvation and for that end, 1 he condescends to Reason with us, 2 to show he loves the doing Christian this is a duty laid at the door of every one that hears the Gospel, for He hath knit these two together Hearing, and Keeping or doing his sayings, and there are Seven ways of doing.

DOING 1. That is doing upon the back of hearing to make us more conformed to Christ.

2. That we aim at the fulness of the Stature of perfect ones in Christ : Be ye perfect as your Father which is in Heaven is perfect, laying a sure foundation to build on.

3. That we have a new walk, Spiritual mindedness Rom. 8. 1, Phil. 3. 20, Acts 9. 31, Mic. 6. 8, 1 Pet. 1. 16. There must be three harmonies in our walk.

HARMONY 1. Betwixt the duties of the first and second table of the Law.

HARM. 2. Betwixt Light and Practice.

HARM. 3. Betwixt Gods part and our own part in doing they must not cross one anoy^r, for we often aim at Gods—leave our own undone, and, when we win any length, take all.

DOING 4. We are to mark all our Successes and give God the Glory, and mark our Shortcomings and take to ourselves the shame and mourn over them before Him.

DOING 5. We are to be more affected with the Bands that lye on our Spirits than with our want of the Blessing, embracing and dandling on Christ's knees. Our doing must have these Five motives cleaving to it.

MOTIVE 1. It must be timeous. Our heart should be no sooner warmed w^t hearing but our feet should be at practice. I will run the way of thy comand: when Thou hast enlarged me.

MOTIVE 2. It must be orderly Doing. We must begin with Substantials & put circumstantials in their own place. Psal. 119. 'Order my goings in thy way & I shall keep thy testimonies to the End.'

MOTIVE 3. He'll not be kept back from doing neither by friends nor foes. Gal. 1. 16 'He consulteth not with flesh and blood.' Acts 21. 13 'I am ready not only to be bound but to die' saith Paul to his friends endeavouring to keep him back from Jerusalem.

MOTIVE 4. He does constantly. Psal. 119. 32 I will run the way of thy com. q^n thou hast enlarged me.

MOTIVE 5. It has four pieces of Spiritual Wisdom in it.

SP. WISDOM 1. Is, he prizes any attainment he gets and blesses God for it & undervalues himself as Luke 17. 10 'I am ane unprofitable serv^t.'

SP. WISDOM 2. He gives Ch. sayings a room in his heart 'I have hid thy words in my heart.'

SP. WISDOM 3. He gives Ch. the chief Room, Ch. chair is ay at the head of the table then he hath three words to hear 1 Lord what will thou have me to do. 2 Lord help me to do. 3 Not unto me &c.

SP. WISDOM 4. He take Ch. March Stones and Dykes to walk by.

The question may be asked, Were men any better a couple of hundred years ago than now? were these tremendous sermons, the jealous supervision of the Kirk-Session, the penalties that followed on the infraction of its rules, productive of good fruit?—and to that the most contradictory replies may be given.

An age but slightly earlier, that preceding the Restoration, has been spoken of by some as the golden age in the history of our Church's piety, while a reference to contemporaneous

chroniclers only would furnish material for drawing the very
opposite conclusion.   On the one hand, we are told that not an
oath was to be heard, not a child was to be found but could read
its Bible, not a family in which the worship of God was not
observed,[1] while, on the other, a contemporaneous chronicler
writes in 1650: 'Much falset and scheitting at this time was
daily detectit, by the Lords of Session, for whilk there was
daylie hanging, skurging, nailling of luggis, and binding of pepill
to the Trone, and booring of tongues, so that it was ane fatal
yeir for fals notaris, and witnesses as daylie experience did
witness, and as for uncleanis and filthyness, it never did abound
more than at this tyme.'[2]

It is therefore very difficult, indeed impossible, to draw any
definite conclusion as to the actual state of the religion of the
mass of people then, and, as regards the precise period now
under review, we have almost less light to guide us.   In place of
making any such attempt, let us place the Rev. John Williamson,
Dainty Davy's eldest son, in the witness-box, and see what he has
to say for himself as an actor in the times referred to.   During
the time he speaks of, his father was senior minister of the West
Church, after the Revolution.   His confidant, it is perhaps almost
unnecessary to state, was the same whose pages have been
already so frequently laid under contribution, the Rev. Robert
Wodrow.

'He (John Williamson) tells me that when young, and till
twelve or fourteen, he was very rackish; and for all kinds of
tricks, breaking of yards, stealing of fruit, and playing at
games, he was inferior to none, and drew up with coal-stealers,
and such company, only he had still a terror to swear.   Thus he
continued mightily given to game, till through the Latin and
Greek, and he was a semic.   His father was abroad, and his

[1] Kirkton.   [2] Nicoll's *Diary.*

mother-in-law had brought him in a habite of going of family worship in his father's absence, and he had a sort of form, without anything of thought anent it. One day he was very much engaged in a game with his comrades and had lost all that afternoon. They were playing in the Kirk-yeard for money, and the more he lost the more he was engaged to venture, and to continue, and still he lost. Many messages were sent for him to come home, but nothing would part him till he lost all his money almost, and it grew dark. He was wonderfully chafed in his mind, and full of passion and anxiety. When he came in, his mother chid him, and ordered him to take the Bible immediately, and go to worship. He did so, and scarce knew what he read or sung. When he came to pray, his conscience smote him, that he was in an ill case to pray to God. However he went through it with great confusion, and immediately went to his room, and his conscience challenging him heavily that he had gone over light, had mocked God, and taken his name in vain, and was guilty of a sin next to that which is unpardonable. Thus he wrestled and groaned much of the night, till he ran in to the ordinary channell of good resolutions, and promises to amend, and subscribed a personal covenant. This wore off a little as to the terrour, but somewhat still remained, till another conviction came in some time after, and that throughout the work. However, this was the beginning of a good work in him.'[1]

This little bit of personal history is very instructive, and almost suggests a solution of the mysterious discrepancy already referred to between the recollections and the matter-of-fact records of bygone times.

[1] Wodrow's *Analecta.*

D

CHAPTER IV.

ALMOST from the days of the Reformation, the first pre-liminary to the dispensation of the Sacrament of the Lord's Supper was that the members of Session should go through their respective districts, and reconcile all those who were at variance. A notice to this effect appears regularly in the records of Session meetings, down to the time of the Revolution, when the practice appears to have been discontinued. It would however be hardly fair to David Williamson and his Kirk-Session on this account to attribute to them any indifference on such a subject. The explanation is more probably to be found in the fact that, at the time, the nation was in such a state of political and religious excitement, that any such proceeding would have been little better than a farce.

From 1680 to 1700, as for many years previously, the Communion was celebrated once a year, on one or several consecutive Sundays, generally in July or August. Then, as until quite recently, preparatory services were held on the Thursday and Saturday, and a thanksgiving service on the Monday following the actual day of Communion. The principal duty of the members of Session on these occasions seems to have been to attend to the gathering in of the collection, made on behalf of the poor, only a few of their number assisting in the actual dispensation of the Sacrament.

The following notice, relative to that of 1693, might be taken as showing the usual arrangement:—'The Session appoints Jas. Ferguson and John M'Gill to gather the tokens, the last Sabbath of the Communion ; John Davis and Robert Finlay to carrie the bread ; Francis Cuthbertson and William Clark to carie the cups ; George Cramond and James Murdock to attend the cups. All the elders who collected the last four days the preceeding year are to doe the same this year ; the elders and deacons who attend the Kirk doors last year are to doe the same this year.' At the time there must have been about forty members of Session. On this occasion, those who collected did well, the total sum amounting to £1024 Scots. One Fast-day was not made to serve two Communion services. When the Communion occupied two consecutive Sundays there was service in the church on eight days within the same fortnight. It is a pity that none of the references to Communions at this time give any indication of the number of those who participated in its celebration. There is no doubt that in the age preceding this it was customary for those of much more tender years to do so than is now the case. Robert Blair, the eminent Covenanter, reproaches himself for having allowed some superstitious feelings to prevent his partaking of the sacred elements when only in his twelfth year.[1] The tide of religious fervour was now however neither so deep nor so universal in its flow as then. To many an earnest soul, during the earlier portion of the times under review, to receive the Sacrament at the hands of a contemner of the Covenant was deliberately to commit a deadly sin, while some, though it is to be doubted whether many such were to be found in Edinburgh, went the length of saying that the communicating with persons scandalous made those that communicated with them guilty of unworthy communicating.

[1] *Autobiography of Robert Blair,* p. 7.

The risks which the more earnest, perhaps some will call them more fanatical, of the Presbyterians were willing to encounter in order to attend the celebration of the sacred ordinance, at the hands of the ' outed ' ministers, when opportunity offered, is a measure of their unwillingness to take part in its dispensation elsewhere. For these reasons, apart from others even more forcible, to be shortly referred to, it may be assumed that the number of communicants during the period preceding the Revolution was scanty. During these days it is to be feared that the celebration of the ordinance was not characterised by any excessive solemnity. To modern ideas the quantity of wine consumed was out of all proportion to the apparent requirements of the congregation, if the account still in existence for wine, etc. at the Communion of 1687 is to be taken as fairly representative. In it there appears a charge for casting 500 tickets or tokens ; but it is exceedingly unlikely that anything like 500 Communicants were present. The whole sum of the collection for the four days of Communion amounted to no more than £38 Scots, about the thirtieth part of what was occasionally collected only a few years later on similar occasions, and it is but charitable to assume that not more than half the tickets were required. The quantity of wine consumed in the service of the Table alone corresponds very nearly to that required on the same occasion at the West Church at the present day, when there is an average attendance of 2000 communicants ; but it would hardly be fair to dwell too much upon this, as it is a well-known fact that the practice in earlier times was different, in this respect, from that prevailing at present. The quantities of wine used at the Communion services of St. Giles' in the days of the Reformation strike us now as prodigious. A whole puncheon of wine was sometimes insufficient,[1] and it seems

[1] See Appendix to Principal **Lee's** *Church History.*

Accompt The Kirk Session of Sirk Kirk

Be Mr Biggs

Impr to the Kirk ...	08	—	09—0
Item to Mr patrik ...	05	—	12—0
Item to Mr ...	07	—	16—0
Item ...	03	—	12—0
Item ...	00	—	18—0
Item to John Guthrie ...	—	—	02—0
Item to John ...	—	—	18—0
Item to ...	—	—	18—0
Item to ...	—	—	18—00
Item to ...	—	—	13—0
Item ...	—	—	02—0
Item ...	—	—	00—0
Item ...	—	—	8—90
Item ...	—	—	00—0
Item for ...	—	—	00—0
Item for ...	02	—	00—0

Summa is — 3ˢ — 03—0

33 — 16 — 6
1 — 15 — 0
31 — 1 — 0

certain that a much deeper draught of the cup was then taken
than now. The previous reference to the Communion of 1693
would of itself almost show this from the fact that, according to
its arrangements, to each elder carrying a cup another was in
attendance in order to replenish its contents.[1]

The details of the account for 1687 are well worth our
examination, but, in doing this, it is to be kept in mind that a
Scots pint was equal to about two English quarts, that is to
say, to nearly three reputed quart bottles of the present day.
The first item is—' To the Kirk 9 pynts of wyne two pynts of
ale.' What was done with the ale is rather a mystery. About
this time, in the more remote parts of Sweden and Norway, it
was actually used in the dispensation of the Sacrament, but it is
not likely that such was the case on the present occasion, and it
is probable that it was intended for the refreshment of those
who wished it, quite apart from the service of the Table. The
next item is one of 'four pynts of wyne' for the benefit of
the minister who presided, Mr. Patrick Hepburn. The treasurer,
in settling the account, seems to have thought this rather too
much, and has noted on the margin 'two pynts'—that is, six
bottles—'allowed.' The same quantity is charged against the
precentor, but only half (one pynt) allowed. We then come to
the Kirk-Session, whose requirements, after the bad example
set them, seem modest—only four pynts. At the meeting
of Session, a very full one, prior to the Communion, twenty-
three members were present, so that the wyne allowed them
was little more than half a bottle apiece. The next item
is in favour of Will Byers, the beadle,—one pynt; but this,

---

[1] The inventory of the effects belonging to the West Church in 1747, as handed
over on the death of Neil M'Vicar, by his widow, to the surviving minister, is still in
existence. From it we learn that for the Communion Service there was then one
flagon to each cup, there being four of each.

along with one of the precentor's pynts, the treasurer appears
to have struck out,—the reason very likely being that Will
Byers was himself the purveyor of the wyne. He was an
innkeeper, in a small way, and it was his house, in the
vicinity of the church, which was afterwards acquired by Mr.
Williamson as a manse for the junior minister. Presumably
on the principle of not muzzling the ox that treads out the
corn, the tapster who drew the wyne is allowed a pynt, while
the baxter, who brought the Communion bread, got no less than
two pynts of ale, and a chopin, that is to say an imperial quart,
of wyne. In all, no fewer than seven and a half quart bottles
of liquor seem to have been consumed by this creature, and
it is not surprising therefore to see that the following entries
are in favour of the officers of Portsburgh, Potterrow, and
Canongate, each of whom is allowed his pynt of wine. The
two first mentioned were parish officers, and frequently employed
by the Session in the apprehension of offenders against discipline. Their presence seems quite in order, but that of the
Canongate official is not, and would seem to indicate that the
two others, unaided, had found some difficulty in the performance
of their duties. Perhaps the baxter was a strong man, and, if
he drank all that Mr. Byers made the Session pay for, he
would certainly give some trouble.

It is probable that the wine charged against the minister and
precentor was a species of perquisite, and was not consumed at
the time, but there is very little doubt that all the rest was.
That being so, it is rather amusing to find that drinking on
the Communion Sunday was reprobated as a very grave mis-
demeanour. This we see from the Minute following on the
Communion of 9th August, when the following appears :—
'Given to the thesaurer, George McHarper, his penalty, being
4 lbs. Scots for drinking upon the Communion day, and was

exacted in 40 lbs. Scots, if he should be found in the like here-after.'

It is but fair to Mr. Hepburn and his Kirk-Session to say that there is no reason to believe that they were either better or worse than their neighbours. For aught we know, Mr. Hepburn always conducted himself with perfect outward propriety. And this was not always the case. But three years before this the Provost of Stirling complained to the Synod of Edinburgh that Mr. Hunter, the second minister, there had, 'on a Communion day, so intoxicated himself with the Sacramental wine, that, when he tried to preach, he misbehaved, and spoke nonsense.'[1]

It is pretty certain that the wine then in use was Claret. Port was unknown ; in fact, a good many years later Burt declares that there was not one glass to be obtained for love or money in any part of Scotland. As regards Claret, the price agrees with what we know to have been the price according to which it was selling in Edinburgh not very long before. According to a proclamation of Magistrates on 31st May 1667,[2] prices were fixed at—

White Wine, .	12s. the pint.
Claret, .	18s ,,
Rhenische,	36s. ,,
Seck,	40s. ,,

Of the Communions subsequent to the Revolution we have no such interesting peeps. No accounts are in existence throwing any light upon them, while the information in the Minute-books is very meagre. Only one point of interest is worth recording, viz., that, from a passage in the Minute of 27th July 1693, it would appear that, at the Communions then held, provision was made for the participation in the service of what

[1] Fountainhall.   [2] Nicoll's *Diary.*

would now be known as 'occasional communicants.' The entry runs thus :—

'The Session recommends the former method in the distribution of the tokens for the Sacrament to be used, which was the last year, both as to parishioners and *strangers.*'

A reference to the previous Communion throws no further light, which is tantalising, as the arrangement suggested seems out of harmony with the time.

CHAPTER V.

THE subject which, next to the supervision of the morals of the parish, called for the greatest attention on the part of the Kirk-Session, was the care of its poor and the distribution of its charities.

In regard to the poor, the situation of the parish was unfortunate. Its principal divisions were mere suburbs of Edinburgh, and the evil fame of Edinburgh in this respect was notorious and of long standing. Nigh two hundred years previously Dunbar had written—

> ' Your burgh of beggeris is ane nest,
> To shout thai swenzouris will nocht rest,
> All honest folk they do molest
> Sa piteuslie they cry and rame.
>   Think ye nocht schame
> That for the poore hes nothing drest
> In hurt and sclander of your name?
>
> Your proffeit daylie dois incres,
> Your godlie workis less and less,
> Through streittis nane may mak progres
> For cry of cruikit, blind, and lame.
>   Think ye nocht schame
> That ye sic substance dois posses,
> And will nocht win ane bettir name?'[1]

[1] Satire on Edinburgh.

E

It is however to be kept in view that there were but few if any soliciting charity who were not physically unable to earn their bread. That healthy spirit of independence which is so characteristic of our nation is faithfully reflected in the early Scotch penal enactments against sturdy beggars, thiggers, sorners, and such like. Some of these were of terrible severity ; indeed, under one Act, passed in the reign of James II., it would almost appear that a persistent course of able-bodied mendicancy might be construed into a capital offence. Hence the claims of the aged, the helpless, and infirm only had to be considered.[1]

Of these the parish had doubtless far more than its own fair share. Its streets and roads were infested by numerous objects of pity, who had come from other quarters, and had no legitimate claim upon it. Charity should begin at home—so the Kirk-Session thought as far back as 1619, when they enacted that no one should be allowed to solicit alms who had not received a badge from the constituted authorities, the object of the badge being to enable parishioners to identify their own poor, and so prevent any misapplication of their charity. This plan was only partially successful, however, and, in course of time, it became the custom to give to such of the poor as were considered deserving of aid a regular monthly allowance. This allowance varied according to the ability of the Kirk treasurer. The revenue applicable was derived from different sources : from the interest, or, as it was then called annualrent, of various bequests, from fines, sums

---

[1] Beggars were easily satisfied in those days. Burt, writing of them a little later, says : ' Before the Union,' that is to say before 1707, ' they never presumed to ask for more than a boddle, or the sixth part of a penny, but now they beg for a baubee or half penny ; it is common for the inhabitants, when they have none of the smallest money, to stop in the street, and, giving a half penny, take from the beggar a plack, that is two boddles, or the third of a penny, in exchange ;' but he goes on to say, ' Here are no young idle fellows or wenches begging about the streets, as with us in London, to the disgrace of all order.'

received at private marriages and baptisms, from collections, interment dues, etc. The first of these should have yielded a much larger revenue than it, at least prior to the Revolution, did. In the beginning of 1680 the capital stock belonging to the poor amounted to £6600, 13s. Scots, but on this the arrears of annualrent actually amounted to no less a sum than £4000, —a clear proof that the interests of the poor were not very well looked after. This capital sum the Kirk-Session sought to augment in one rather curious way. On the highest authority we are told not to do our 'alms before men, to be seen of them,' but almost in the same place we are also instructed to let our light so shine before men that they may see our good works. Now, with the private interests of the donors the Kirk-Session had nothing to do, but with those of the poor they had a great deal; and, in regard to these, they thought the latter precept much more to the point. They therefore instructed the treasurer to cause to be inscribed, in a suitable place, in letters of gold, the names and designations of those who had mortified money for the use of the poor, that it might serve to stimulate others to follow their good example.

There was apparently but one way of investing the sums thus received, viz., by lending them out on bond, at six or seven per cent. of interest, and in 1680 no less than one half of the little fortune of the poor was lent to the grandson of the unfortunate Sir William Dick of Grange, the greatest merchant, and probably most liberal man, of his time in Scotland.

'Then folk might see men deliver up their silver to the state's use, as if it had been as muckle sclate stanes. My father saw them toom the sacks of dollars out of Provost Dick's window intill the carts that carried them to the army at Dunse Law,' said douce Davy Deans long after; but Provost Dick's liberality to the cause of the Covenant and the Commonwealth did not recommend him to the favourable notice of the Royalists. After the Restoration, the vast sums he had lent to the Government were never repaid, and he died at last, in great misery, in a debtors' prison, having been arrested in London, for a paltry sum, while endeavouring to obtain justice.

By far the most important source of income, after the return of David Williamson, was the collection annually made at the Communion-time. This, then, sometimes amounted to over £1000 Scots, a great improvement on that obtained in the later days of the Episcopal *régime* when the receipts were comparatively trifling—little more than equal to the cost of the Communion elements. Thus in 1687 the collection for the four days amounted in all to £38 Scots, the expense of the service to £33, 7s. In the following year the wine alone cost £28, while the whole collection was but £37.

To make matters worse for the poor, in those days the authority of the Kirk-Session appears to have been at a very low ebb. There was no lack of delinquents, but delinquents either refused to appear before the Session, or, if they appeared, treated the sentence of the Session bailie with indifference. The usual harvest in this shape was not forthcoming; indeed, from July until October but one trifling penalty was paid. In these circumstances, it is perhaps unnecessary to state that the monthly dole to the enrolled poor was not a large one. During 1685 the sum divided averaged £36 Scots a month; by 1687 it had fallen to £27; the average for the following year was but £20, and in its course we come to entries where, after the sum is mentioned, the words appear, 'all that was in the box.'

After the Revolution a different state of matters prevailed. On 10th April 1693 it was estimated that the sum required for the maintenance of the poor that year would amount to £2000

Scots, and by the year 1700 the monthly expenditure had risen to £300 Scots. For the purpose of comparison, the following table has been compiled, from which it will be seen that the revenue was of a very fluctuating nature :—

	1683.			1688.			1699.		
Ordinary Church-door Collections, . .	£390	0	6	£215	13	8	£864	12	8
Collections at Communion-time,[1]	84	11	0	37	0	0	594	16	0
Contracts, Marriages, and Baptisms, . .	135	11	6	46	11	0	24	7	0
Fines,[2] . .	461	9	8	69	19	0	35	6	0
Seat Rents,		...			...		79	10	0
Burial Fees,[3]		...		33	6	8	12	5	0
Donations, . .		...		7	0	0	346	19	8
Interest, . . .	120	0	0	136	17	8	283	0	0
Allowance for Communion Elements, per Bishop of Edinburgh, . . .	84	0	0					...	
Sale of Trees in Kirk yard,		...			...		10	0	0
	£1275	12	8	£546	8	0	£2250	16	4

The regular revenue was, of course, applied to the relief of the poor of the parish mainly, but the practical expression of the sympathies of the church members was not confined within such narrow limits. Although, in the matter of beggars, they had, so to speak, to act on the defensive, in other matters their

[1] The collection at the Communion of 1699 is very much less than was usually obtained at this time, that of the previous year being £1111, 2s. To some extent this may have arisen from the large sums given for behoof of the poor at other times during the year as donations.

[2] The sum realised from fines in 1688 would have been much larger had all the fines which were imposed been paid.

[3] The sum at the credit of 1688 was a single fee: '50 merks received from Rot Malloch for the Interment of the corps of the Lady Damhead in the Kirk;' that for 1699 arose from the sale of 'turffes' at the rate of 14s. Scots each.

charity was distributed in a most catholic spirit, while the sums raised for special purposes seem to have been very much greater in proportion to the actual wealth of the congregation than is now the case. Charity then, more frequently than now, was the result of a direct personal interest. It dealt more with the needs of the body than with those of the soul, and it was all-embracing in its scope. The persecuted Protestant Churches of the Continent, the relief of Turkish galley-slaves abroad, the building of bridges and harbours, and assisting of such as had suffered from the ravages of war or of famine at home, each in turn profited by its exercise, while, in the case of parishioners, misfortunes such as the loss of a leg, the existence of such diseases as cancer, were a sure passport to its aid. Apprentice fees were sometimes paid in whole or in part by the Session, and special collections made from house to house, within the particular district, in order to secure the benefit of professional skill for those unable to pay for it themselves.

It is perhaps travelling beyond the proper bounds of the present subject to refer to these special charities in detail, but one or two of the principal among the earlier may be mentioned, as the subject is interesting. The first subscription of note referred to in the records was in 1609 for the great bridge at Perth, which took eighteen years to build, and was swept away within four years of completion. In 1622, £800 Scots was subscribed for the distressed Protestant Church in France. In 1631, 672 merks were collected for the ministers of the Reformed Church in Bohemia. In 1645 Argyllshire was harried by Montrose, and towards the loss sustained by its inhabitants the West Kirk contributed 432 merks. Two years later 525 merks were collected for the inhabitants of Orkney, then suffering from famine.

These sums are very large if compared with the stipends of the ministers. That of David Williamson, on his appointment in 1661, was but 600 merks, only one half of the sum sent, forty years previously, to the distressed Protestant Church in France. The purchasing power of money was immensely greater in those days than now. For the board and maintenance of an Aberdeen Professor, when engaged on College business at Edinburgh, the sum of £2 Scots was then allowed per diem.[1] A similar allowance at the present day would probably be the same sum in sterling money ; multiply that by 400, and we get an idea of the worth of the contribution to the Church of France at the present day. Such evidence points clearly to the fact that the spirit of our forefathers was the very reverse of what, according to a certain school of writers, it has been depicted. In those days Scotland was probably the very poorest country in Christendom. It had no manufactures, and but little commerce. The struggle for existence was hard, the average income low, and yet we see proofs of a generosity which need certainly fear no comparison with that of the present day. Nor did the burghers of St. Cuthbert's, as is a complaint of common occurrence now, forget the claims of those at home in their zeal for the welfare of those abroad. In 1681 no less than 456 merks were collected for the benefit of those who had suffered the loss of household plenishing through a great fire which had devastated a part of the Potterrow.

The following entries from the treasurer's accounts, which show the way in which he dispensed the funds at his disposal, apart from the claims of the enrolled poor of the parish, may fittingly close the chapter. They might be repeated indefinitely :—

[1] Arnot's *History of Edinburgh.*

1684.

Sept. 4.	Given out to a poore distressed man, Wm. Jack,	£2	18	0
	,,	to a poore woman, Elizabeth Douglas, who broke her leg, ...	0	14	0
	,,	to Jonet Milkim, who is blind, lame, and deaf, ...	0	14	0
	,,	to a poore orphan lying in a fever,	0	14	0
	,,	to John Stewart's distressed sick wife,	0	14	0
Oct. 8.	,,	to a distressed schoolmaster, . .	1	3	10
	,,	to a poore German, ...	0	14	0
	,,	to Isobel Smith, a poore distressed gentle-woman, ...	1	8	0
	,,	to two distressed parishioners in Ports-burgh, ...	1	8	0

CHAPTER VI.

CHURCH DISCIPLINE.

No notice of the ecclesiastical features of the period now under review, no matter how brief, would be complete which did not refer to what was known as ' Discipline.' The very books in which the Minutes of the Kirk-Session meetings were engrossed were known as Discipline Books, and with good reason, for, with all due deference to Mr. Sime,[1] it may be safely asserted that, whether the Presbyterian or Prelatical party were in power, nineteen-twentieths of their contents at this time will be found to consist of matters connected with the exercise of the functions of the Kirk-Session, as guardians of the moral wellbeing of the parish.

That it is impossible to make people sober by Act of Parliament is now accepted as a truism, but what the early fathers of our Church aimed at, in their fiery zeal for a reformation of all kinds, was something far more difficult. The powers then intrusted to the Church were ample, most ample; if they did not include the power of life and death, they included practically everything else. Twice during the history of Presbyterianism they were wielded by a body of men, as able, as energetic, and

[1] ' Throughout the whole period of Episcopal rule little else is to be found in the records but fines and imprisonments, a detail of which would sicken rather than gratify the reader.'

as filled with a burning desire after the highest good, as ever guided the councils of any other Church. That the efforts of Knox and Melville at the first, of Henderson and Gillespie, and Bruce and Baillie, at what has been called the second, Reformation, were not altogether successful, is a proof that the system of what may be called punitive legislation in Church government has been tried and found wanting. The space required for the full discussion of such a subject would, however, far exceed the modest limits which have been assigned to the present work. The sole reason why the matter is referred to at all is the fact that it was within the period whose most salient features we are now considering that the Church was shorn of her ancient powers. When William III. first took the reins of government in hand, the future of the Church of Scotland hung wavering in the balance. That Episcopacy was then detested in the Lowlands of Scotland is of course incontrovertible, but the superiority of the Lowlands, in respect of wealth and population, was not nearly so strongly marked then as it is now. It was an important part, but only an important part, of the country. Doubtless throughout broad Scotland there were very many more Presbyterians than Episcopalians, if all were told, but they were by no means in the overwhelming majority which it has now become the fashion to assume. Aberdeen was staunchly Episcopal ; its citizens were not likely to forget the bigoted intolerance of the Covenanters, and the means they used to propagate their creed ; and the same feelings existed more or less in the north of Scotland ;[1] excepting of course the wide districts throughout

---

[1] ' Wodrow gives an instance of this a good number of years after the Revolution. According to him, the minister of Aberlemno for two years could get no one to attend his ministrations, his parishioners, without exception, attending a form of service which had been set up, conducted by an Episcopalian.'—*Wodrow Correspondence*, i. 223.

which the faith of Rome was still dominant. The strength of Episcopacy there is very clearly brought out by the fact that, in the first General Assembly held after the Revolution, that of October 1690, in a house of one hundred and eighty members, not a single representative was from the north of the Tay.[1]

On the one hand, William saw a compact body of Episcopalians, through storm and sunshine faithful to the reigning monarchy; on the other, a mingled mass of Presbyterians, of all shades of opinion, fiercely hostile to one another, many of whom, and by no means the least active, a long series of cruel wrongs had made fanatical and almost fantastic in their opinions as to the respective powers and provinces of Church and State, whose opinions were far more consistent with an adherence to a republic than to the form of government which it was his wish to establish. Had the Episcopalians selected a more politic and straightforward envoy to plead their cause with him than Bishop Rose,[2] had Presbyterianism had a less powerful advocate in William's councils than Carstares, the Revolution Settlement in its present shape might never have been effected. The Episcopalians suffered then for their unfaltering loyalty to perhaps the most worthless monarch who ever sat on the throne of Great Britain. That their loss was Scotland's gain, that it was a

[1] Cunningham.

[2] Previous to Rose's interview with William III., he had seen Compton, Bishop of London, who gave him the following message : ' The King bids me tell you that he now knows the state of Scotland much better than he did when he was in Holland ; for while there he was made to believe that Scotland generally all over was Presbyterian, but now he sees that the great body of the nobility and gentry are for Episcopacy, and it is the trading and inferior sort that are for Presbytery. Wherefore he bids me tell you, that if you will undertake to serve him to the purpose that he is here served in England, he will take you by the hand, support the Church and your order, and throw off the Presbyterians.' To this Dr. Rose answered that his instructions did not extend so far, and that, as for himself, he would rather abandon all than renounce his allegiance to James. ' In these circumstances,' said Compton, ' the King must be excused for standing by the Presbyterians.'—*Cunningham.*

righteous retribution for all the miseries which they had been indirectly instrumental in drawing down upon the Presbyterians for the previous twenty years, will probably not be called in question by the bulk of Scotchmen at the present day; but let us not forget that the Episcopal Church of that day must not be identified with the illiterate base-born hirelings intruded upon the parishes of the outed Presbyterian ministers. Its pastors were very far from being all unworthy. If it is responsible for a James Sharpe, it can also point to a Robert Leighton.

The struggle was only nominally between Presbyterianism and Episcopacy. What cared Middleton or Lauderdale, Turner or Dalziel or Claverhouse, about the form of church-government? Their mission was to crush all resistance to the Crown. It happened in Scotland to become identified with Presbyterianism, and so the will of the monarch was identified with Episcopacy. The struggle had begun with an act to which Lowland Scotland can point with pride—the almost universal surrender of house and home, and nearly everything that the world counts dear, by those who filled its pulpits, rather than soil their conscience by ignoble surrender to the State. It closed at this time in a way not unworthy of the high beginning. By an almost unexampled instance of self-restraint, the curates were permitted to depart in peace. Poor feckless creatures! commissioned to proclaim the glad tidings of 'peace on earth and good-will to men,' their principal occupation in but too many instances had been to play the spy upon their own parishioners, for the benefit of such hell-hounds as Grierson of Lag and Johnston of Westerhall. How many a one rotting in the dungeons of Dunnottar, or sweltering as a slave amid the swamps of Barbadoes, had had cause to curse them with his dying breath! how many wives had been made widows, how many children fatherless, through their instrumentality!—and yet when at last the hour of deliverance came, not a single life was lost, or retributive act of vengeance taken upon them. Like so much unclean chaff they were shaken from their places, and departed, to hide among the slums of the larger towns, and pray for the return of that illustrious defender of the faith, King James II.

William III. was therefore in a manner shut up to espouse the cause of Presbyterianism, but, in doing so, he took one step which must have been very much to the satisfaction of his Episcopal subjects in northern parts. This was the passing of an Act, in his first Parliament of 1690, whereby all Acts denouncing civil pains upon sentences of excommunication were rescinded. On these Acts the whole system of punitive church-government was founded. The effect of this was not much felt at first, the force of public opinion was so strong, but it gradually told, and in the course of time it was seen that the Church was willing to accommodate itself to the change. The passing of sentences which could not be enforced was plainly incompatible with its own dignity. Sackcloth gowns became things of the past, and even the practice of publicly rebuking offenders in presence of the congregation, long before the expiration of last century, was, so far as the West Church was concerned, a matter of ancient history. To the Episcopalians, of course, the relief was immediate. Presbyterian public opinion was nothing to them. In the past, if they refused to sign the Covenant, they risked the forfeiture of their whole goods and chattels to the State, but now they could set the most peremptory commands of the Church at defiance. True, as yet the public observance of the forms of their Church was proscribed, but that did not affect their individual liberty. In matters religious it was unbounded.[1]

[1] The public performance of the Episcopal form of worship was authorised by Statute in 1712.

With such weighty matters as the passing of sentences of excommunication we have however nothing to do at present. During the last twenty years of the seventeenth century the records of the West Church do not furnish us with a single instance. The offences dealt with by the Kirk-Session were, in most cases, breaches of some one or other of the Statutes of the civil law against profaneness. The enforcing of these was specially intrusted to kirk-sessions, who, however, as kirk-sessions, were not supposed to possess the power of inflicting civil punishment, this being a matter pertaining to the session bailie, whose powers were most ample. By fines, the jougs, by imprisonment, and by banishment from the parish, the guilty were kept in awe. The offences dealt with were various, but by far the most numerous were minor breaches of the seventh commandment, after which came Sabbath-breaking. A perusal of the records would seem to show that there was more open vice prior to the Revolution than afterwards, and that during the former period, especially towards its close, there was less respect paid to the authority of the Kirk-Session.

Mr. Williamson and his colleague, however, did not trust solely to the efficacy of their pulpit admonitions, or the more perfect surveillance of their Kirk-Session. They went on the principle that prevention is better than cure, and they made use of a very potent means to that end, which under their predecessors had in great measure gone to sleep. This was the power given under an Act of Assembly of 1648, whereby all new-comers to a parish were bound to produce testimonials from that which they had left. If a stranger could not produce such a testimonial, the bailie would be requested to 'exclude him the street'—in other words, to turn him out of the parish. As a rule, this was unnecessary. When the certificate which had no existence was demanded, there was generally one excuse or another for delay in its production, till, finding subterfuge unavailing, the defaulter took himself off, and the parish knew him no more. By this means the intrusion of an injurious foreign element was to a great extent checked.

With a view to showing as precisely as is now possible the state of the parish at this time, an analysis is given below of the discipline cases before the Kirk-Session in 1681, when the Episcopal *régime* was in force ; in 1691, when Presbyterianism was fairly re-established ; and again in 1699, at the close of the period under review. The numbers refer only to cases where *actual appearance was made* before the Session—a fact which must be kept in mind, as offenders, sometimes by keeping out of the way, and at other times by a persistent ignoring of its citations, occasionally set the Session at defiance. In so doing they ran the risk of being put out of the parish by the presiding magistrate, and this not unfrequently happened.

	1681.	12 months, 1691-2.	1699.
Impurity,	27	34	18
Sabbath-breaking,[1]	7	16	20
Drunkenness,	4	...	...
Scolding and swearing,	5	5	3
Resetting bad characters,	1	1	4
Irregular Marriages,[2]		1	4
Contemning Fast-days,	...	2	...
Abuse of Session,	2		...
Beating of Father,	1		...

As already said, less respect was paid during the earlier portion of this period to the authority of the Kirk-Session than after

[1] This generally refers to drinking or entertaining during hours of Divine Service. The heinous offence of carrying milk to town was also frequently under the notice of Mr. Williamson and his Session.

[2] Generally speaking, an irregular marriage was where the ceremony had been performed by an Episcopal minister.

the return of Presbyterianism to power. It is not easy altogether
to account for this, but it is pretty certain that it did not arise
from any general antipathy to the existing state of things. The
indifference of Edinburgh to the cause of the Covenant was
notorious, and is again and again reprobated by the author, or
authors, of *Napthali.* 'Wretched Edinburgh' she is called, and
told that, as she exceeded London in her sins, so she deserved
London's plagues and judgments. One thing is certain : it was
then very difficult to obtain the services of a strong kirk-session.
More than once notices appear of the refusal to serve of those
elected elders and deacons. On one occasion, indeed, several
of these combined to set the Session at defiance, and, so
far as can be seen, did so with impunity. The average
attendance at meetings of Session was much smaller. In
1681 it met fifty-five times, the average attendance being
under ten. In 1699 it met forty-five times, the average
attendance being over twenty. Even the average of ten
in 1681 was entirely due to the fact that on several occasions during the year matters of great interest occurred,
when, through the attendance of the principal heritors, who
seem mostly to have been elders, the numbers swelled to
over twenty. From 6th October to 8th December the average
attendance of seven meetings held was under five. It is also
but too probable that the five who thus acted as guardians
of morals were not by any means exceptionally suited for
the position. One thing is certain, that the active members
of Session in 1688, when the curtain fell, were not members
of the new Session, when it rose in 1691. Of thirty-nine
elders and deacons who attended the first meeting, that of 4th
June 1691, the names of but two are familiar, both of them
being large heritors.

It will be noticed from a reference to the table, that drunken-

ness was comparatively rare,—rare to a degree hardly compre-
hensible, in an age so little removed from that of 'the Drunken
Parliament' of 1662, when the Lord High Commissioner and
his crew had drunk to the devil's health at midnight, at the
Cross of Ayr; but that it was rare among the lower and middle
classes would seem to be certain if the evidence of the
Discipline Books is to be accepted, and there is no reason why
it should not. Kirk-sessions were specially intrusted with the
duty of putting in force the laws against profaneness, under
which head drinking to excess and at untimeous hours, along
with other delinquencies, fell to be classed; and this duty they
did perform, and on its performance no mean part of the
revenue of the Church depended. What, then, is the explanation? If the vice, unhappily so common now, had no existence
then except among the higher classes, how did this arise?—and
to this the answer must be, that, at the time, intemperance was
an expensive luxury. 'As drunk as a lord' is a phrase full of
significance. Whisky was then unknown. True it is that
reference will be found to Aqua Vitæ and Strong Waters in
Acts of Parliament passed about this time, but, going to the West
Kirk records of the twenty years in question, not one single
notice of either appears. Now, if Aqua Vitæ was then in anything like common, or even occasional, use, it almost certainly
would have been referred to. One of the offences falling most
frequently under the cognisance of the Session was that of
entertaining during hours of Divine Service, and the notices of
pynts of ale and chopins of wine are innumerable, but not one
instance of the other is to be found.

One of the most curious features in the system of Discipline
as then exercised was this, that, in cases involving a public
rebuke, the offenders, before such was given, required to find

caution that they would give full and complete satisfaction to the discipline of the Church, and pay whatever penalty should be imposed upon them, under a penalty sometimes as high as a hundred pounds Scots. In the event of caution not being forthcoming, as often as not the offender was *at once* referred to the Justice of the Peace, to be *imprisoned* until he found the required security. Than such a proceeding surely nothing could be more harsh or unreasonable, and yet it was of frequent occurrence. One is tempted to ask the question, What became of those who could not find caution? how long were they thus detained? But to that no answer can be got. Caution being forthcoming, the next consideration was payment of the fine, and, as a rule, it was only after this had been paid in full that offenders were permitted to 'enter upon their satisfaction,' that is to say, their course of public rebukes. During Episcopal days it was possible for wealthy offenders to get off, in almost every case, with a Sessional rebuke, by the payment of a heavier fine, but it was not so after the Revolution. If the occasion called for it, no contribution, however large, *ad pios usus*, could purchase exemption from the misery of having to 'satisfie' in public. These public appearances were but rarely insisted on, excepting in the case of a particular class of sins. According to Fountainhall, it was not used for 'drunkenness, swearing, Sabbath-breaking, lying, and other enormities,' but in this he is not absolutely correct. An instance in point occurred in 1693, in which one Archibald Gilmour, for swearing and drunkenness, was rebuked in public.[1] Perhaps the explanation of the unusual severity was the fact that he had, as credibly reported, said 'Damn the Whigs,' and of course this was a very grave offence.

In the consideration of such customs we are but too apt to

[1] West Kirk Minutes.

I Robert Andersone Wright & Burges of Ed: binds
& oblidges me that Agnes Simclar _____ nt James
Lyon sergent shall give full & compleat satisfaction
to the discipline of the Church of St Cuthberts &
pay ye penaltie the session of the sd Church shall think
fit to enjoyn, And that againe the terme of Witsunday
nixt And that under the pain & penaltie of a hundered
pounds scots to be payed by me to the o+hers of the said
Church for the use of the poor in caise of faild & non=
performance of the premisses agt the sd terme And for
the mair securitie I am content & consents that thir pnts
be insert & regrat in my judges books competent within
this kingdome that lrs & exe+is of horning may pass hir
wpon on ane simple charge of six dayes attourney etrw
hoirto constitute _____ my pross &c
In witnes qrof I have sett thir pnts wt my hand
at Brigto the twintie second of Apriell Ja Vyr eightie
seven years Befor thir witness mr Jon Wishart wryter
hoirof and Gilbert Dick wryter in Ed:
                                        Robert Andersone
                              Jo Wishart witnes
                                  Gil: Dick witnes

assume that the men of those days were of a coarser fibre, and less sensitive than we should be to the humiliation involved in such penalties. Probably it was so, but not to the extent generally supposed. Of this the records furnish us with one notable example. In September 1693 Wm. MacMorran, a cobbler, confessed to a grave breach of morals. He was appointed to 'buy ane sack goun to stand in at the kirk door, and to appear before the congregation on Sabbath next.' At the following meeting of Session it was reported that MacMorran had obeyed its behests. His punishment was however not over; he had many more similar appearances to make, but before these could be overtaken the man went mad. On the 12th October it was reported to the Session that he had 'turned distempered,' when the Session requested his elder to make inquiries. This was done, and at next meeting it was reported that 'MacMorran's wife could not get him kept in the house, and that the neighbours were feared for him in the night-time.' In these circumstances it might have been expected that the Session would remit the rest of his punishment, but they did nothing of the kind; on the contrary, the Session-Clerk, after giving the above details, gravely records the fact, 'the Session delayed him for a time,'—for all time, as it proved, for the man had become a raving madman, and his name does not again appear.

Cases of this kind used to be spoken of as 'Cutty-stool Cases,' from the name popularly given to the stool of repentance, the seat usually occupied by offenders; but, so far as can be ascertained, the West Kirk never had a cutty-stool. In 1591 a pillar had been set up, at which the guilty had to stand. Pillars were in vogue at that time, but in these matters, as in everything else, there is a fashion, and by the time now spoken of stools of repentance were in fashion, and the Kirk-Session, having a praiseworthy desire to keep pace with the times, resolved to have one erected in the church. The usual place for this was just below, but facing, the precentor's desk, and just at the distance at which the thunders of the pulpit would be most effective ; but the Session, considering that the older custom of having offenders 'placed on high' was preferable, deputed two of their number to 'speak with the deacon of the Taylours anent a plaice at the east end of their loft for a stool of repentance.' To this, however, the 'Taylours' had a wholesome objection, and positively declined to entertain the proposal, so that any idea of making a change was abandoned, and offenders continued to be rebuked at the pillar as before. It may be asked, by those curious in the matter, What exactly was a cutty-stool ? and to that no precise answer can be given. It was not a stool, however ; that is certain. According to Burt, it was fashioned like an arm-chair, and was raised on a pedestal nearly two feet higher than the other seats, directly fronting the pulpit, while Mr. Edgar tells us that during the latter days of the old church of Mauchline 'it was just a common pew, a little exalted above its neighbours, and situated on the left hand of the pulpit.' That it was fixed, and capacious enough to accommodate several at a time, also appears from references in Lamont's Diary. From him we learn that Cromwell's soldiers took great delight, when in Fife, in pouring contempt on the whole institution. At Largo, and other places, they sat on the cutty-stool during time of sermon, while in Kirkcaldie and Kinnowhie they pulled them down. That they did so merely from dislike to the custom, as being of Presbyterian origin, and not from any sympathy with the vice principally aimed at, is probable. Their own discipline while in Edinburgh was pretty stringent. In place of a fine, and three rebukes in public, they would in similar circumstances have got a whipping and 'three doukis in the sea.'

The duties of the Kirk-Session in matters of discipline were not confined to a mere adjudicating upon the cases brought before them. They were in a manner judge, jury, and prosecutor in one, and even something more. That they acted as a species of ecclesiastical police is notorious, and their alleged prying interference in this capacity has served to wing the shaft of many a sarcasm, launched at the expense of the Church. But the ideal aimed at was something far higher than is generally recognised. According to that, it would seem as though every parish was a diocese, every minister a bishop, and every elder, *minus* the power of dispensing the Sacraments, a minister. Here is what John Welsh of Irongray says in one of his sermons preached in the parish of Cathcart : ' It is a day (the Day of Judgment) wherein we must reckon for all we have done, for every minute and moment of time we have had ; a day wherein the minister must reckon for those of his flock, the parent for his children, the *elder for those of his quarter.*'

This high ideal was however but too easily lost sight of. Doubtless there have been epochs in the history of the Church of Christ, when men suitable for the exercise of such functions were to be found, when the hearts of all beat so completely in unison, that, in the performance of their duties, such office-bearers would have earned only gratitude ; but it is to be feared such epochs have been few, and, looking at it from the present point of view, the only wonder is that some of the peculiar features of the institution were tolerated at all. Take, for instance, a resolution of the Kirk-Session arrived at at their meeting of 19th April 1694 :—

' The Session appoint an intimation to be made from the

pulpit upon Sabbath next, that when elders and deacones goes through to search their bounds, whoever shall keep their doores closs, and not give access, shall be holden as guiltie.'

That is to say, there might be the very best of reasons for declining the honour of a visit from the elder, but to decline it entailed the privilege of a Sessional rebuke, as, in that case, it was assumed that you were guilty of Sabbath-breaking.

CHAPTER VII.

BEFORE referring more particularly to the visitation of the Church by the Presbytery of Edinburgh, it is right that some explanation should be given of its origin prior to the period under review, the custom having now fallen into disuse.

Although almost, in one form, coeval with the institution of Presbyteries themselves,[1] it is probable that, as practised later, it was the work of the celebrated Assembly which sat at Glasgow in 1638. The nation was then in a state of wild ferment. The determined assertion of the Royal prerogative in matters religious had met with an equally determined opposition, and the greatest and best of the nation had bound themselves to stand or fall together in defence of Presbyterianism. The Solemn League and Covenant was sworn to on the flat gravestone in Greyfriars Churchyard on the 28th February of that year, and what

---

[1] At the outset the visitation of churches was conducted, not by the whole Presbytery, but by one or two of their number specially appointed for that purpose. The practice seems to have been the outcome of a very pertinent question put by King James in 1581, through his Commissioners, to the Church : ' In caice the Kirk damned the office of Bischops,' what was to be put in their place? The visitation of Kirks was not especially mentioned then, but, a year later, the following enactment was passed : ' Ordaynis every Presbyterie, within their own bounds, to try the ministers of the same, and if any offences beis found, to punische the same according to the qualitie and estate betwixt and the next General Assembly of the Kirk.'—*Booke of the Universall Kirk.* An interesting example, probably the first on record, of a visitation conducted in this manner, is to be found in the Miscellany of the Wodrow Society (i. 459), where an account is given of the visitation of the kirk of Holyroodhouse in 1583.

followed in the General Assembly at Glasgow was but the natural corollary. By it the fabric of Episcopacy, which King James and his successor had been laboriously rearing during the previous thirty years, was thrown down as in a moment, the bishops were one and all deposed, not merely from their bishoprics, but even from the office of the ministry, and on Presbyteries was devolved in great measure the discharge of their functions. An Act was then passed, to this effect: 'That visitation of particular kirks within presbyteries be made once every year, and that thereat care be had, among other things, to try how domestic exercises of religion are exercised in particular families, and what means there are in every parish in landward for catechising and instructing the youth.' In supplement of this a further resolution was arrived at, forming one of the sixteen 'Remedies' suggested by the Committee, appointed in 1646, for considering 'the Enormities and Corruptions observed to be in the Ministry, with the remedies thereof.' It runs thus: 'That accuracie be used at the visitation of kirks, and that the elders, one by one, the rest being removed, be called in and examined upon oath upon the Minister's behaviour in his calling and conversation.'

This later enactment, perhaps above all others, proves the intensity of the desire then existing among the leaders of the Church for a thorough reformation, in the widest application of the word, throughout the length and breadth of the land. They recognised that such a reformation must begin with themselves. Their own order, that its purity might be recognised as above suspicion, was to be subjected to the ordeal of the most searching inquiry, in the hope that thereafter, through its ministry, the healing waters from the gospel stream might gradually permeate every corner of the land.

However praiseworthy the motive, the means adopted ap-

pear in the light of the present century to be utterly abomin-
able. For this measure the supreme genius of the Covenant,
Alexander Henderson, cannot be held responsible. He was at
the time engaged at Newcastle in his celebrated controversy
with Charles I., as to the respective merits of Episcopacy and
Presbyterianism. A prominent member of the Assembly was
the Rev. Andrew Cant, of whom poor Spalding complains so
piteously in his *Memorials of the Trubles*, and it looks very
like a bit of his handiwork. So far as can now be ascertained,
the fruits realised were of the most meagre description. The
principle, so beautifully illustrated in Holy Writ in the story of
the woman taken in adultery, is one which is not confined
to race, or clime, or century. 'He that is without sin among
you, let him first cast a stone at her,' must have been often
heard in spirit in the time of these visitations ; and many a
good thumping lie told in consequence, as being, in the choice
presented, the lesser evil. Evidence of this is seen in the records
of the Presbytery of Strathbogie, which contain numerous
detailed accounts of visitations which took place about this time.
With one exception, the result of the elders' examinations was
nought, their sworn depositions generally amounting to neither
more nor less than a stereotyped admission of satisfaction. The
one exception referred to occurred at a visitation held at
Grange in 1649, in which certain grave charges were made
against the minister by *one* elder. The minister was ultimately
deposed, but the investigation which was held disclosed the
fact that between the minister and the elder there existed a
bitter feud ; but for this, it is all but certain that nothing would
have been heard of the faults of the former.

During the period under consideration, more than one
presbyterial visitation occurred, but these are only briefly
referred to, as what then took place was in a sense outside the

H

ken of the Kirk-Session, and fell to be narrated in the records
of the Presbytery of Edinburgh. These for this period are
unfortunately no longer in existence. The illustration of
this peculiar institution which follows is therefore taken from
them at the nearest point in time available, viz. the 14th June 1711.
The visitation then held took place very much at the instance
of the Kirk-Session, who wished to bring some influence to bear
upon the heritors, who were delaying in a scandalous manner to
attend to their duties in the matter of repairing the church,
which was getting into very bad order.

Only the first part of the Minute, which is of great length,
occupying seventeen folio pages, is given. The latter portion,
which refers to the repairs of the church, is less interesting, the
result being that the Presbytery ' thought fit to discern the heritors
of this paroch in the sum of 2000 merks, to be paid by them pro-
portional to their several valuations.' This the heritors appear to
have tacitly agreed to. By this time, it would seem that the
practice of taking the separate depositions of the elders on oath
had been discontinued.

·VISITATION OF PRESBYTERY.

'At the West Kirk, Thursday the 14th June 1711, *ante
Meridian :*

'The Presbytery of Edinburgh did convene within the West
Kirk of Edinburgh, alias St. Cuthbert's, for visitation according
to a former appointment thereanent, and, after sermon by
Mr. Thomas Paterson, one of the pastors of this paroch, upon his
ordinary text,[1] Romans vi. 12, the congregation removed, and
after prayer the roll was called, and there was found present
Mr. John Steadman,—*Moderator ;* Masters William Carstares,

[1] See page 19.

John Webster, John Flint, Robert Sandilands, William Hamilton, Robert Taylor, Thomas Paterson, Samuel Semple, James Grierson, John Messon, William Millar, Neil M'Vicar, Walter Allon, David Malcolm, John Guthrie, John Mathieson, John Webster, Matthew Wood, and John Fleming,—*Ministers ;* John Blair, Writer ; David Dundas ; Robert Elliot, Chirurgeon ; William Baillie, Wright ; George Warrender of Lochend, and James Findlay,—*Ruling Elders.*

'Mr. Thomas Paterson, being inquired if he had given timeous advertisement of the meeting of the Presbytery this time and place, in order to a parochial visitation, according to order thirty day of May last. He answered that upon the third of June current, the presbyterial act appointing the meeting was read from the pulpit, and intimation made according thereto, and also letters were written to the non-residing heritors ; whereupon he was removed, and the opinion of members being asked concerning the doctrine delivered by him this day, he was unanimously approved therein, and being called the same was intimated to him. All being removed except members, Misters Thomas Paterson and Neil M'Vicar, Ministers of this Paroch, were asked the following questions :—

'1st. Have you an eldership, and what is the number of your elders and deacons, and have they district bounds assigned them for their more particular inspection ?

'2nd. Are the members of your Session grave, pious, and exemplary in their lives and conversation ?

'3d. Do they worship God in their families ?

'4th. Are they careful in their attention on public ordinances and diets of Session ?

'5th. Are they careful and impartial in the exercise of their respective offices ?

'6th. Do they visit families ?

'*7th.* Have all the elders subscribed the Confession of Faith as enjoined by the Acts of the General Assembly?

'*8th.* How do the people profit by your ministry? and

'*9th.* Are they obedient to Church Discipline?

To which questions it was answered that there is an Eldership in the paroch, and that their usual full number is twenty-four elders and twenty-four deacons, but that at present they want three of that number by reason of the death and flitting of some of the members of Session, but others are to be chosen in their room; and that the elders and deacons have their district bounds assigned for most part. As to the second question, answered in the affirmative, and that the members of Session are very encouraging to their ministers. As to the 3d, 4th, 5th, 6th, and 7th questions, answered in the affirmative. So far as the ministers can learn, only some few of the elders have not yet subscribed the Confession of Faith, having been absent when the rest did it, but are ready to do it. As to the 8th and 9th questions, answered by the ministers that there is not such success by their labours as could be wished for, yet they are hopeful their labour is not altogether in vain, some having reformed their lives, and all do submit to Discipline, except a very few who prove obstinate, but in such cases they were either referred to the Presbytery or to the Civil Magistrate.

'The ministers having been removed, the elders and deacons were called in, and the following questions put to them, viz.:—

'Does your ministers preach sound doctrine, so far as you understand the Holy Scriptures and our Confession of Faith?

'*2nd.* Do they keep much at home, attending on their ministry and are they diligent therein, or do they occasion to themselves unnecessary diversions therefrom?

'*3d.* Do they lecture and preach in the forenoon, and preach again in the afternoon every Lord's Day by turns?

' 4*th.* Do they read a large portion of Scriptures every Lord's Day, and expound the same?

' 5*th.* Have they a week-day sermon?

' 6*th.* Are they frequent in catechising their parishioners?

' 7*th.* Do they preach catechetical doctrines on the Lord's Day?

' 8*th.* Do they administer the sacrament of Baptism in an orderly way, when the congregation is convened, or privately?

' 9*th.* Do they frequently administer the Sacrament of the Lord's Supper in their congregation, and do they carefully keep from that holy ordinance all who are known to be scandalous, grossly erroneous, or ignorant?

' 10*th.* Do they visit the sick, and pray over them?

' 11*th.* Do they visit families in a ministerial way, teaching and admonishing from house to house?

' 12*th.* Do they keep Sessional meetings frequently, and are they impartial in the exercise of Discipline against offenders, and is the Session's diligence therein recorded in a book?

' 13*th.* Do the ministers keep family worship? are they grave, pious, and exemplary in their lives and conversations, and do they rule well their own houses?

' To all which questions the members of Session answered that they had nothing to complain of their reverend ministers in these things, but were well satisfied with them; and that they are diligent in their work of preaching, lecturing, and catechising; and as to Sessional meetings, they keep the same every week for most part, and sometimes oftener; that they have a week-day sermon the whole year over, and do give the Sacrament of the Lord's Supper once every year; and because of the multitude of communicants, they take two Sabbaths, one after another, for celebration of the Holy Ordinance.

' The ministers having been called in, they and the members of Session were jointly asked the following questions, viz. :—

' *1st.* Have you a register of the proceedings of your Session in the matter of Discipline, and your other actings ?

' *2nd.* If there be a register of Baptisms and Marriages kept in the paroch ?

' *3d.* If there be a magistrate in the paroch for putting in execution the laws against profaneness ?

' *4th.* If there be pains taken to see if the worship of God is performed in families, and to have the ignorant instructed ?

' *5th.* If Testimonials be required from persons who come to reside in the paroch ?

' *6th.* If there be any Papists or others who join not in the communion of the Church residing in the paroch ?

' *7th.* If there be frequent meetings of the Session for prayer, fasting, and conference, according to the seventh Act of the General Assembly of 1699 ?

' *8th.* Are the deacons careful of the collection for the Poor, and if there be any mortification for pious uses in the paroch, is the same duly applied ?

' 9. Have you a kirk treasurer, and what is the poor stock at present, and what are the maills belonging to this church ?

' 10. Have you a Kirk Bible, Confession of Faith, Acts of Assembly, the Queen's Proclamation against Profaneness, with the abridgment of the laws against Immorality ?

' And it was answered : 1. That they do keep exact Registers of Discipline, which have been produced to and given out by the Presbytery to be revised, and they now produced before the Presbytery those Registers following, viz., Imprimis, a Register of Discipline beginning 20 Nov. 1584 years and ending 20th Mch. 1594. Item, another beginning 28th Augt. 1595 and ending

12 Oct. 1648 * * * (*as on margin*). Item, a Register of Baptisms, in answer to the second question, being produced, beginning the 7th day of January 1565 and ending 4th Augt. 1577. Item, a second Register of Baptisms begining the 1st April 1596 and ending 29th Dec. 1642, the two preceding Registers of Baptisms being in the same book. Item, a third, etc. Item, a Register of Marriages, etc. etc. To the third question it was answered that there are several Magistrats, Justices of the Peace, and Baillies residing in, and frequently holding Courts in the Paroch, and the Session as need requires do apply to them for executing the Laws against Immorality and for suppressing vice. To the 4th it was answered that heads of families are exhorted to worship God therein, and it's to be feared many do neglect the same, yet there are some who do perform that duty. To the 5th it was answered that Testimonals are called for, as is enjoined by the Acts of Assembly. To the 6th it was answered that there are some few Papists and also Quakers in the Paroch, and others also who do dissent from this Church, residing in the Paroch, but they are but few in comparison with them who attend the dispensation of Gospel Ordinances. To the 7th question it was answered that the work of this Session is very great, and they have so frequent meetings and long sederunts that they have not hitherto had stated meetings for fasting, prayer, and conference. To the eighth question it was answered that the Deacons do carefully collect for the poor, and distributes to their necessities according to the Session's orders, and there was produced a Register of Book of Accompts of Collections and Distributions 19th October 1648, and ending 18th May 1655. Item, a Register of the penalties of scandalous persons payable to the Church and Collections, 30th Nov. 1648 to 8th Augt. 1661, etc. etc. To the 9th question it was answered that Dr. James Forrest

19th Oct 1648 to 19 Nov 1667.
17 Sept. 1674 to 13 Mch. 1679.
13 Mch. 1679 to 6 July 1682.
9 July 1682 to 29 July 1686.
5 Augt. 1686 to 22 July 1688.
4 June 1691 to 30 Jany. 1696.
6 Feb. 1696 to 9 May 1700.
16 May 1700 to 5 Feb. 1708.

of Wester Grange, one of the Heritors of the Parish, is Kirk
Tresaurer, who has the custodie of this Churches stock with the
Bonds belonging thereto, and that one of the Members of Session
assists in calling in and giving out the Churches money in
smaller sums, and the said Dr. Forrest, being called, was required
what the present stock belonging to the Poor does now amount
unto; and he answered that when he entered it was 12,596 merks
Scots, and that it is now 13,000 merks, but there is about 500
merks thereof which is not well secured. And as to Mortifica-
tions, the Session answered there is none belonging to this
Paroch at the Session's management, nor know they of any in
the hands or management of any other in the Paroch. As to the
uttencills of the Church, it was answered that the Session hath
four silver cups with their cases. Item, a silver bason and
Lavor, four peuther flagons, six pouther basons, a brass bason
and a little peuther one, eight communion table cloaths. Item,
ten little cloaths for the bread, collecting, and baptism. Item, a
green cloath for the Session table, a green pulpit cloath with
silk fringes, six wanscot stools for the Collections. Item, a tent for
the Church yaird at Communions, a Chist in the Minister's house
for holding the cups, Basons, and other uttencills above written.
Item, a Beer for burying of poor strangers. To the tenth
question it was answered that there is a Bible, Confession of
Faith, a Copie of all the printed Acts of the General Assembly
of this Church, begining with the year 1638, and ending with the
year 1710, and the Queens Proclamation against Immorality,
Abbreviate of the Laws against Prophanness, and also the
Abridgement of the whole Acts of Parliament belonging to the
Session ; but the Bible is not in the Session's hands.'

CHAPTER VIII.

THE NISBETS OF DEAN.

I.—SIR PATRICK NISBET.

DURING the last twenty years of the seventeenth century the references to different members of this family are very numerous. An offshoot from the better-known family of Nisbet of Nisbet, it was descended from Henry Nisbet, whose son William was more than once Lord Provost of Edinburgh in the reign of James VI. Their family residence was a venerable mansion overhanging the Water of Leith, which was demolished so recently as 1845, in the course of laying out the grounds of the present Dean Cemetery. From the material which has come down to us, a volume, and by no means a small one, could be filled with the history of the relations exist-ing between different members of the family and the Kirk-Session: the perpetual warfare, on one subject or another, waged with Sir Patrick the father; the alternate vain-glory and shabbiness of Henry, the eldest son; and the repeated tribula-tions of that sad scapegrace, Patrick junior, his younger brother. Alike in the pages of Wodrow and of Mr. Sime, we see Sir Patrick depicted as an interesting sufferer in the cause of Pres-byterianism, while a too hasty appreciation of the terms of Henry Nisbet's epitaph, as it still appears on the north side of the present church, would present him, in our imagination, as one ever straining after those ideal heights of perfection which are in symbolism pictured to us by the poet in 'Excelsior.'

I

The race has long been extinct, as Wilson in his *Memorials of Edinburgh* tells us, and hence there is no reason why the truth should not be spoken of its representatives at this time, and mention made, in some detail, of the great case, 'The West Kirk Poore *v.* Sir Patrick and Harie Nisbet,' especially as it is, next to the Revolution and its consequent effects, by far the most interesting episode of the period we are now considering.[1]

It was hardly fair in Mr. Sime, after his strictures upon the Episcopal ministers of the West Church, to deal so gently with Sir Patrick Nisbet, because he favoured Mr. Williamson, as no one could know better than he that Sir Patrick was not exactly of the stuff that martyrs for the truth are made of. If he was to refer to him at all, he might have given him a slight share at least of the obloquy he dispenses in other quarters.

The main dispute between Sir Patrick and the West Kirk Session arose in this way. For seven years previous to 1680 the funds belonging to the poor of the parish had been intrusted to the care of one Alexander Shed, a maltster in the little township of Water of Leith. During this period no account of his intromissions was rendered by him. Latterly it became known that he was heavily embarrassed, and a majority of the Kirk-Session were clamant for the appointment of a new treasurer. The removal of Shed did not however suit Sir Patrick's interest, and he strenuously opposed it. In this he was supported by Mr. Gordon, the minister, over whom he seems to have had some control, and by several other members of Session, tenants of his own, and, like Shed, completely subservient to his will. In this position of affairs, the more independent members sought the assistance of the Bishop of Edinburgh, who decided in favour of a new treasurer, who was thereon appointed.

In the course of Shed's treasurership there had been lent to

[1] See Note on page 82.

Nisbet, from the poor's stock, the sum of 2000 merks, Shed being, in his turn, according to accounts presented, even more heavily indebted to Nisbet. When it was evident that Shed was in difficulties, Nisbet was not slow to take advantage of the position he held, so as to protect his own interests. Apparently Shed was at first rather unwilling to comply with his wishes; at least there seems to be no other way of accounting for the Rev. Mr. Gordon's appearance in the matter; but with the latter's tacit consent, Shed gave Sir Patrick an acquittance in full of his indebtedness to the poor, receiving from him presumably a discharge *pro tanto* of the debt due by himself to Sir Patrick. The latter's claims against Shed amounted to very much more than this. He already at this time held Shed's personal bond for £4600 Scots, and now in security thereof he obtained from him a heritable bond over his property in the Water of Leith, which, by an assignation, he prudently transferred to his eldest son Henry. Matters were further complicated by the fact that Shed, who seems to have been completely overwhelmed with debt, had also granted, about the same time, other bonds over the same property to other of his creditors, the result being a tremendous amount of litigation.

Considering the lapse of time which has taken place, the number of papers still in existence referring to the matter is remarkable, but still all insufficient to admit of our fully ascertaining the results. It would seem, however, that, at the finish, as at the beginning, the struggle lay mainly between the Nisbets and the West Kirk poor, and, that being so, we may ignore the existence of other creditors, and revert to matters as at the date of the appointment of the new treasurer, Mr. James Eleis of Stanhopesmilnes. That gentleman lost no time in seeking to undo the evil work of his predecessor, and at once raised two different actions,—the first against Sir Patrick Nisbet, Mr. Gordon,

and Shed, for the purpose of obtaining a reduction of the discharge of Sir Patrick's debt to the poor, which Shed, acting in
collusion with the others, had fraudulently granted ; the second
for the purpose of proving that Shed's bond for 2500 merks, the
amount of the deficit shown by his accounts, which he had
granted in favour of the poor over his lands in Water of Leith,
was entitled to precedence over that granted by him, about the
same time, over the same subjects to Sir Patrick.

The former of these actions was soon settled in favour of the
poor, but the latter proved to be a much more tedious affair.
The counsel retained by the Kirk-Session was none other than
Sir John Dalrymple, afterwards Earl of Stair, and, for all future
time, infamous on account of the share he had in the Massacre
of Glencoe. He took up the position that Nisbet, by the very
fact of his being a member of Session, and thereby a guardian of
the interests of the poor, was precluded from doing anything in
the way of preferring his own interests at their expense ; and, in
addition, not merely brought out the fact that, in the execution
of the assignation which he had granted in favour of his son,
there were several gross irregularities, but even offered to prove,
by means of the clerk who had extended it, and one of the
witnesses thereto, that at the time of the execution of the
assignation, the heritable bond to which it had reference was
not in existence, and that the one now produced had been
fraudulently antedated.

This was a very serious charge, especially when brought forward by one who happened at the time to be Lord Advocate.
At the present day, it would probably lead to an early settlement
of the case at issue by the immediate disappearance of the de-
fendant, but in those good old days it was otherwise. Whatever
might be his other faults, Sir Patrick was not deficient in personal
courage. He stopped Mr. Eleis on the public highway, and after

storming at him in pretty much the same style as Mr. Chucks the boatswain was wont to do in *Peter Simple*, told him that, if he and his witnesses deponed as they had promised, he would nail both his and their lugs to the Trone—the penalty at the time for falsehood.

Mr. Eleis resented such treatment very keenly. He brought the matter under the notice of the Kirk-Session at their next meeting, and craved redress. That the Session had been insulted in the person of their treasurer was but too apparent. Such conduct could not be tolerated, and it was remitted to the presiding minister to instruct the Session's agent to take immediate steps to obtain redress. Nothing, however, was done; indeed Sir Patrick, apparently in order to mark his contempt for the whole of them, attended the very next meeting of Session, when the matter was allowed to drop. The doughty Knight had evidently gained his end, for, knowing what was in store for them, Mr. Eleis's witnesses did not come forward, and the charge of antedating the bond had to be dropped. The case was again and again before the Court, until, on the 18th February 1682, it decided that, although right in point of law, Sir Patrick had used indiscreet means for getting himself preferred to the poor of the West Kirk, and therefore ordained that the poor should come in equally with him, and the maills and duties be divided equally betwixt them. In this position the matter rested until the beginning of 1687, when Sir Patrick, on what grounds it is impossible to discover, raised an action for the purpose of reducing the claims of the West Kirk poor upon Shed's estate. No papers have come down to us in regard to this second action, and no reference is made to it by Fountainhall, but there is little doubt but that in it Nisbet was finally successful. His purse was probably a good deal longer than that of the Kirk-Session, and in those days justice was regularly bought and sold. Of this, in this very case, proof still exists.

Of the papers referring to this period which are still in existence, perhaps none is more interesting than the statement by Mr. Eleis of his outlays in the case, a reference to which will show that Mr. Eleis and the West Kirk Session were no better in this respect than their neighbours. Sir David Falconer and Sir John Foulis of Ravelston were judges in the case, one of the interlocutors, still in existence, being signed by the latter; and here we see that the former was paid, through his servant, in all £2, 18s., while the son of the latter received £1, 9s. The purity of the Scottish bench was then very far from being above suspicion ; indeed, it has been asserted that the judges appointed by Cromwell during his jurisdiction were the only ones of the age whose decisions were received with respect—a fact not indeed disputed by one of their less immaculate successors, who, nettled at some invidious comparison made in his presence, angrily retorted, 'Deil thank them ! a wheen kithless loons.'

According to the writer of the humorous poem on the subject in *The Court of Session Garland*, it was the custom then for each judge to have a retainer, who was known as his 'peat,' whose good offices suitors found it desirable to obtain. Sir David Falconer, it was alleged, was especially greedy and distrustful. He was, shortly after this date, in 1682, raised to the dignity of Lord President, under the title of Lord Newton, and this is the way in which he is alluded to in the poem, the assertion made regarding him being amusingly borne out by what we have before us :—

> 'My Lord Newton, a body that gladly would live,
> Is ready to take whate'er men would give,
> Who wisely considers when "peat" to himself
> He avoids all danger of parting the pelf.'

Ane accompt of qt money the jont thesaurer
Hath expended for persueing the proove
And persewing Sir Patrick Nisbet

		lib	s	d
Octob 15 1679	ffor instrument money to Robert Burnet	002	09	00
nove. 27th	ffor consulting Sir John Dalrimple	026	16	00
Ditto	To the sd Sir John his servant	002	16	00
ditto	To mr David Gray, James Edmingston & mr David his servant	006	18	08
Decemr 17th	To mr David Gray, his cley & to James Edmingston	006	09	04
Ditto	Given to James Hay qn mr Gordon & sd deponed	002	18	00
4 Januar 1680	Given to mr Roderick mKenzie	002	18	00
7 Januar	To Sir John Dalrimple for drawing a Bill	011	12	00
Ditto	To the sd Sir John his two servants	004	07	00
Ditto	To mr James Dalrimple Clerk	005	16	00
8 Januar	To mr wm Chiflies servant for writing	002	16	00
Ditto	Given to Sir Jon Dalrimple to draw and informe	014	10	00
Ditto	To Sir John's servant	002	18	00
Ditto	ffor writing 14 doubles of the informations	004	04	00
12 Januar	To Sir David ofalckonars servant	001	09	00
Ditto	ffor instrument money qn Sir pa: refused to depone	000	13	04
21 Januar:	To James Edmingston qn Sir pa: was reexamined	002	18	00
Ditto	To James Edmingstons servant	000	18	04
27 Januar:	ffor writing the 3 papers conting additionall answers	000	13	04
28 Januar	To Sir David ofalckonars servant	001	09	00
2 febr:	To Comissar Foulis sone for his appearance	001	08	00
Ditto	ffor summonding Sir Patrick to hear sentence	000	08	00

Summa — 096 : 00 : 00

The sums given in the present case seem incredibly small to be given to such important personages in such a way, and it is probable that Sir Patrick Nisbet would have little difficulty in presenting more weighty arguments of the same nature for their consideration. The account is interesting in other respects, and deserves a careful inspection. The irregularity of the sums paid is only apparent, as it would appear that at this time fees were calculated neither in pounds nor merks, but in dollars; either rix-dollars at £2, 18s., or leg-dollars at £2, 16s. Thus the first fee given to Sir John Dalrymple was 6 leg-dollars; the second, for drawing a bill, 4 rix-dollars. In this way young Foulis got half a leg-dollar, and Sir David Falconer's servant two half rix-dollars.[1] Henceforward the lands of Alexander Shed remained in the possession of the Nisbets, and in the valuation-roll for 1726 Patrick Nisbet, Junior, is entered as proprietor of Alexander Shed's land in Water of Leith, rated at £110.

After about ten years, more or less, spent in the fight, the result seems to be that its honours were equally divided. Sir Patrick's own private debt, of which Shed had fraudulently discharged him, was again secured to the Session, but, on the other hand, he had established his preference in regard to Shed's estate, and, so long as that remained, their postponed security for £2500 was practically worthless. The West Kirk Session were a forgiving body of men. Notwithstanding the insult offered to them, in the person of Mr. Eleis, in the end of 1681, at a very full meeting of Session, held on 6th December 1683, at

---

[1] The number of coins, both of gold and silver, current at this, or at least at a period not very much antecedent to this date, was very great. A table of these is given in Balfour's *Annals*, entitled, 'A Table of Money as it is to pass through the Kingdom of Scotland,' conform to Act of Parliament of March 1651. In it no fewer than twenty-one gold and thirty-one silver coins are mentioned, the values of the former ranging from £3 up to £17 Scots, of the latter from £3, 6b. 8d. Scots down to 2b. 2d., or about 2¼d. sterling.

which Mr. Eleis was present, the Laird of Dean was unanimously elected thesaurer for the coming year, and no fault
is to be found with the way in which he discharged his
duties. His behaviour in 1687 was however so distasteful to
them as to produce a coldness, which led to his leaving the
church, and joining the congregation formed at this time by Mr.
Williamson. Their meeting-house, according to Mr. Sime, was
in the vicinity of the Dean, and, if so, it is pretty certain that it
was set up there with Sir Patrick's consent, if not assistance.
It is proverbially unsafe for those who live in Rome to quarrel
with the Pope, and in espousing the cause of David Williamson this was practically what Sir Patrick did. Archbishop
Paterson was now all-potent. He was not the man to forget
how Williamson had openly, from the pulpit of the West
Church, preached against his order, and set the whole Episcopal
hierarchy at defiance. Besides this, had he not some years
previously personally interested himself in behalf of the poor,
and, by insisting on the appointment of a new treasurer in
room of Alexander Shed, in great measure interfered with the
successful accomplishment of Nisbet's ends? We can well
imagine that he felt doubly aggrieved at the latter, and in the
mishap which now befell him, it is at least probable that the
Archbishop's hand had a share.

One Mushet was at that time 'reider' at the West Kirk. He
appears to have resented the erection of Mr. Williamson's meeting-house very keenly, as it not merely emptied the church on
Sundays in time of service—that was the minister's grievance, a
merely sentimental one ; but it was rapidly becoming the scene of
most of the marriages of the congregation—that was the 'reider's'
grievance, a more substantial one, doubtless, as it interfered sadly
with the ingathering of such fees and perquisites as were going
on such occasions. Once, if not twice, Mr. Williamson was

arrested on frivolous charges brought by him. These led to no result, but Mushet[1] was more successful in regard to the accusation he brought against one whom, next to Mr. Williamson, he no doubt considered most blameworthy in the matter. This was our friend Sir Patrick, who was reported by him to have spoken slightingly of some Acts of Parliament, and to have alleged that the Presbyterians had as many Johnstons as the Prelates had Jardines. We can imagine the doughty Knight treating such a charge with perfect indifference. To one who had been formally accused of perjury,[2] and again of fraud, before the highest Court of the land, by men of position, it was a small thing to answer for. But for some occult influence, no attention would at such a time have been paid to so frivolous a matter, —for it was now July 1688, the last martyr of the Covenant had bled and died, and soon the eastern gales would be wafting the sails of the Prince of Orange to Torbay. Conciliation to the disaffected all round, to all but the stern Society men, was the order of the day, and there seems no reason why Sir Patrick Nisbet should have been treated with exceptional severity. His fine is the very last recorded by Wodrow. Had he allowed matters to rest as they were, and been content to share such pickings as Shed's estate afforded with the poor, there would have been no occasion for him to leave the church in 1687, and it is probable that he might then have expressed the opinions he did with perfect impunity: neither Mushet nor even Archbishop Paterson could have done him much harm. As it was, Alexander Shed's lands cost him dear, for the fine levied upon him by the Court amounted to no less than £5000 Scots.

His suffering so severely, ostensibly in the cause of Presbyterianism, would doubtless incline men to think forbearingly of

[1] See Appendix B.   [2] See Appendix C.

his previous misdeeds ; and although he was no longer able to dominate in the Session when that body, as reconstituted after the Revolution, resumed its meetings, it is still quite clear that he was treated with very great respect. Thus we find on one occasion that a member of the congregation was rebuked for allowing Sir Patrick and another to remain drinking in his premises during time of Divine Service, but nothing is said to indicate that any censure was meted out to the principal offender himself.

Unfortunately, Sir Patrick got into a much more serious scrape not long after, in the autumn of 1695. By this time he must have been a pretty old man. Thirteen years previously his eldest son had presented him with a grandchild, but his heart was yet youthful, and beat responsive to the charms of the fair. Our old friend Will Byers, whose pynt of wine had been disallowed by the Kirk thesaurer at the Communion of the summer of 1687, was still beadle, and still gave entertainment to man and beast at his little hostel near the old West Church, and there Sir Patrick turned in to refresh himself one afternoon in the month of August 1695.

Now the attractions of the little hostel were not confined to the superior quality of the liquor sold. In addition, there were the personal charms of Mrs. Byers, which, according to what was then said, must have been considerable. She and the Knight, who seem to have been old cronies, fell to discussing matters which had taken place two-and-thirty years previously. The theme had proved a fascinating one, and the Knight had perhaps stayed rather longer than there was occasion for, or than he would have done had he known that there were two lady friends of Mrs. Byers in the room above, with their ears glued to some chinks in the floor, drinking in every word that was uttered.

That she gave him one, two kisses for 'auld lang syne,' and

then told him that they would cost him some Holland to make toys (caps) with, was proved. That she said she never used anything but Holland at £4 the eln was also proved ; and all this was of course going rather far—further, probably, than Will Byers would have approved of—but there was no great harm in it after all. The scandal the affair caused was however tremendous. Mrs. Byers had made no secret about the kisses, and the Laird and she were cited to appear before the Session, there to be confronted by the witnesses. Sir Patrick of course appeared, and appeared in high dudgeon. He stormed at the witnesses; they were not, he said, worth the King's onlaw, and utterly untrustworthy ; then he left the meeting, and refused to attend any more.

The whole matter was supremely ridiculous, but there seemed to be no end to it. Of Sir Patrick, as of Wordsworth's tinker, it might probably be said,

> ' Full twenty times was Peter feared
> For once that Peter was respected ;'

and, either from the one cause or the other, elders kept aloof. One meeting of Session was held after another, without a sufficient number of members being present to dispose of such important business, and at last, in despair, the Kirk-Session, on the 21st November, resolved to refer the affair to the Presbytery. Whether it ever actually reached the Presbytery is doubtful, but unfortunately this cannot be ascertained, as the records of the Presbytery of Edinburgh for the period are no longer in existence. Had they come to any deliverance on the subject, it should, as in similar cases, have been intimated to the Session, and referred to in the Minutes : henceforward, however, on this subject they are blank, and it is probable that the matter went no further. The edifying spectacle of Sir Patrick's public repentance, along with the beadle's wife, which had doubtless been looked forward to, and in anticipation enjoyed by every Mrs. Grundy for miles around, was not to be.

The Session, considering the fuss they had made at the outset, appear to have made an ignominious retreat in showing such forbearance, but doubtless they knew their own affairs best, and their forbearance had its reward. A few months later we find rather a startling announcement in the Minutes of 28th May, and that to the following effect :—' This day report was made that Sir Patrick Nisbet offered 2000 merks, for the debt due to the poor be the deceast Alexr. Shed, and also that the papers belonging to the said Alexr. his land were offered to be considered by the Session.' We shall not be so ill-natured as to speculate whether this was cause or effect of the Session's forbearance, or whether, indeed, the two things had any connection with one another. One thing certainly deserves to be noted, and that was the remarkably cool way in which the Kirk-Session received the news of Sir Patrick's generous offer. They had no claim on him in the matter. Accounts between them had been finally cleared long ago ; and, at the least, one would have expected some expression of gratitude—but no, the matter was simply referred to the thesaurer, and other business taken up. The thesaurer, Mr. Adam Gairn of Greenhill, did not forget that Shed's debt was not 2000, but 2500 merks, and he apparently thought that if the Session forgave the arrears of interest they would do quite enough. With Sir Patrick's consent, the matter was referred, July 5, 1697, to Sir John Foulis of Ravelston and Mr. Jas. Lewis of Merchiston, and by them, as announced at the Session meeting of 31st March 1698, it was decreed that Sir Patrick should pay to the poor 2500 merks, in full satisfaction of all they could demand from the late Alexander Shed his land.

After this Sir Patrick is heard of rarely. He paid his 2500 merks in due course, and the last occasion on which we hear of him is as one of the Committee for the clearing of the treasurer's accounts in 1708. His extraordinary signature, for his *P* was a work of art, appears at the foot of the docquet of 22d March of that year.

II.—HENRY NISBET.

HENRY NISBET of Dean, Sir Patrick's eldest son, was, in his own right, one of the most considerable heritors in the parish, and at an early age took a keen interest in its affairs. He was under age at the outset of the great litigation on the subject of Alexander Shed's lands in 1680, yet in 1687 we find him appointed Kirk treasurer. In this capacity he proved no better than some of his predecessors, to say the least. So far as can be seen from the statements made on behalf of the poor, in the litigation referred to previously, and not disputed, Sir Patrick had conveyed his whole right and title to what might be found belonging to him of Shed's estate to his son. At the very least it may be assumed that the father could not move in the matter without the son's consent, and yet the time of Henry Nisbet's treasurership is the very time that is selected for the later litigation, of which we know nothing except that it appears to have been successful.

Henry Nisbet's treasurership lasted one year. His predecessor, Gilbert Robertson of Whitehouse, had held office for four, while Hunter of Muirhouse, who succeeded him, occupied the post for three years; and a fair inference is that the same cause which induced Sir Patrick to leave the church for David Williamson's meeting-house operated here also, and curtailed the period of his son's treasurership. The Kirk-Session had seen enough of the Nisbets to allow either the wolf or the wolf's cub to remain guardian of the flock, and so his tenure of office was short. At the close of the inventory of the securities belonging to the poor with which his account closes, the following curious entry appears: 'Item, there is the ballance of my accompts to be lent out, £666, 13s. 4d.' Of this sum Henry Nisbet appears to have lent himself, probably *had* lent himself, one half. His successor, Mr. Hunter of Muirhouse, left his accounts in admirable order, and from them we learn that Nisbet gave a bond for that sum on the 5th July succeeding, but that interest thereon was charged from the preceding term of Candlemas. The legal rate of interest at the time was only six per cent., and this rate we find charged on other bonds mentioned in the same statement. Nisbet, however, on the 500 merks he had lent himself, was paying interest at nine per cent., a fact pregnant with the suggestion that there had been something not quite clean in the transaction, and that he was being squeezed in consequence.

It was now, however, that the great event of the Revolution took place. Sir Patrick Nisbet had been fined an enormous sum for his supposed sympathy with the cause of the Covenant. Sir Patrick's previous misdeeds were forgotten. He was a species of martyr, and a reflected glory shone upon his son. They had been, in a manner, sent to Coventry by the old Kirk-Session, but when it was reconstituted, they only of the former members seem to have been asked to join it, and, as if still further to obliterate any unpleasant recollections, Henry Nisbet was again appointed its treasurer, and for another year took charge of the interests of the 'Poore.'

Into his further achievements in that capacity it is unnecessary to enter; indeed, but too much space has already been

devoted to them in the past. Our interest in Henry Nisbet
arises from another cause altogether. He appears to have been
a very mean man, but, singularly enough, along with this, he was
possessed of the most egregious vanity, and to this circumstance
it is that we owe the one link which connects the old West Church
with the present edifice. Let us be grateful to him accordingly.
Of the importance of his family he had the most exaggerated
ideas. We find him on one occasion protesting at a public
meeting that the Nisbets of Dean were entitled to take precedence of all other heritors in the parish, and, in the close
of 1691, it occurred to him to accentuate their importance by
the erection of a family burial-place of imposing appearance.
Nearly fifty years previously the same idea had been enter-
tained by his grand-uncle, Sir William Nisbet of Dean, who had
then obtained a grant from the Kirk-Session of a suitable site.
This grant had been in a manner cancelled through lapse of
time, and in November 1691 Henry Nisbet applied to the Kirk-
Session for its confirmation, which was granted, as also leave to
open up a quarry in the churchyard for stone for its construc-
tion, the only condition being that he would, in recognition of the
favour, give a suitable gratuity to the poor. This was agreed to,
and the work forthwith set about,—set about with rather too much
speed, the Session thought, for in the middle of February they
had to instruct the suspension of the work until the gratuity
was paid. A month later Nisbet paid the gratuity, viz. £39, 10s.
Scots, and the work was allowed to proceed. On the 16th
June the matter was again brought before the Session. He
had failed to keep his promise, to fill up the quarry with good
earth, and the treasurer was instructed to have it done at his
expense, unless done by himself without further delay. At the
time he was presumably a wealthy man, for only at the previous
meeting of Session his father's indebtedness to the poor had

been brought up, and it had been resolved to insist on immediate payment unless Henry Nisbet became security. Of course
Henry Nisbet would do nothing of the kind.

In addition to the erection of the tomb, Henry Nisbet had
also done something by way of further exaltation of the
Nisbets of Dean in the interior of the church,—whether an
'isle' or only a 'loft' it is not easy to say. His work, whatever it was, had left a lot of rubbish in the kirk, which,
with perfect consistency, he left to others to remove. This
we learn from an application made by him, in November,
for the key of the church, in order that he might have the
Nisbets' coat of arms carved in stone above his burial
vault. This was granted, on condition that the expense the
church had been put to in clearing away the rubbish was made
good. Presumably he at once complied with this, as the coat
of arms duly appeared, and now forms the solitary mural
decoration of the present church. During this time the masons
and others employed by him were vainly seeking to obtain payment, and at last, in despair, they struck work, and applied to the
Kirk treasurer, who, after more than one application had been
made to him, brought the matter before the Session on the 26th
January following. Part of the work was then unfinished, and
the Session resolved that, if Henry Nisbet would neither pay
the men nor finish the work, they would do both, as matters
could not be allowed to remain as they were. This they eventually had to do; of course it was understood that they would
shortly be repaid. But year after year passed, until at last, in the
end of 1699, the Session would stand it no longer. They raised
an action for repayment against him in the Sheriff Court, and
obtained decree for the sum expended, viz., £60, and this he
actually paid in the following April.

It may be asked, Why this detailed account of a mean man's meanness? and the reply is that it is absolutely necessary, for the perfect appreciation of the inscription on his tomb, which is still to be seen, though now almost illegible, above the entrance to the vault on the north side of the present church. This inscription has taken its place, with others, in nearly every important work upon Edinburgh which has appeared, from that of Maitland down to the three interesting volumes on Old and New Edinburgh recently published by Messrs. Cassell.

The inscription is in Latin, which, in Maitland's *History of Edinburgh*, is rendered thus :—

'Henry Nisbet of Dean, preferring Fame to Riches, and Virtue to Fame, despising earthly things, and aspiring after Heavenly enjoyments, being mindful of death and waiting for the resurrection, in his own life, and at his own sight, caused build this sepulchral monument for him, in the year of our Lord 1692.'

Perhaps he was possessed of a fund of quiet humour, which he was willing to exhibit, even at his own expense. If so, the inscription was a hit ; for there is something irresistibly comical in the spectacle of Henry Nisbet Sunday after Sunday, for seven long years, admiringly surveying this description of his own virtues, in the happy consciousness that his indifference to riches had been published at the expense of others. Perhaps, however, he may have believed that the picture which he thus drew of himself was true enough to life. In any case, it must for long have proved a fertile source of amusement. The last we hear of him is in April 1699, when he was found to have been drinking, during hours of Divine Service, along with his brother Patrick. Patrick came up for his rebuke at once. The interior of the Session-house was quite familiar to him ; he had been fined a hundred merks only a week or two

L

before for a more serious offence ; but Henry had to be cited three several times before he would attend. It must have been hard for one of his lofty aspirations to appear in such a position, but appear he did, when he was rebuked and fined just like any ordinary sinner.

[NOTE.—One of the original documents in the case ' The West Kirke Poore *v.* Sir Patrick and Harie Nisbet' was presented by the Kirk-Session of the West Church to the Society of Antiquaries of Scotland, when a short notice of the dispute and its final settlement was read by the present author. He has now to thank the Society for their courteous consent expressed through Dr. Anderson that it should be inserted in a more detailed form on the present occasion.]

APPENDIX.

.

APPENDIX A.

VALUATION OF THE WEST KIRK PARISH IN 1699.

	£	s.	d.
Adam Gairns,	0231	16	00
Mr. Robert Byer's heirs,	0128	13	04
John Gairnes,	0179	10	00
Lylburne,	0095	15	00
Mary Cousland,	0032	05	00
Mr. James Reid,	0083	15	00
Penman at Pleas.,	0045	04	04
Adam Thompson there,	0128	13	04
Neuington at Mounthooly,	0074	08	00
John Daling, Pleas.,	0007	06	08
John Davie there,	0026	01	00
Shiens,	0328	00	00
Grainge,	1108	06	08
Bruntsfield,	0286	07	08
Whitehouse,	0307	13	04
Rigland,	0025	00	00
Ploughland,	0495	00	00
Thomas Begsland,	0197	06	08
Greenhill,	0103	16	00
Mr. William Livingstone's heirs.	0025	04	00
Robert Adamson's heirs,	0017	00	00
Andrew Brown, Blackfoord,	0250	00	00
Braides Maines,	0250	00	00
Barronie of Braid,	0800	00	00
Gorgie Milnes,	0207	10	00

	£	s.	d.
Mr. John Muir's heirs,	0083	08	00
Merchistoun, .	2231	00	00
Sir Patrick Hepburn's,	0040	05	00
Elizabeth Napier, .	0017	07	00
Wrights houses,	0352	10	00
Craighouse, .	0252	14	00
Stenhoopsmilnes, .	0478	13	04
Orchardfield Stirling,	0259	13	04
Coats, .	1385	10	00
Craigleith,	0900	00	00
Innerleith,	1940	00	00
Warristoun,	0603	00	00
Bonningtoun,	1015	00	00
Pilrig, .	0900	00	00
Meggatland, .	0225	00	00
Mr. David Watson.	0013	06	08
Dalrie, .	1327	00	00
Gorgie, . .	0450	00	00
Meldrum's heugh, . . .	0192	06	08
Mr. Robert Colt, Trinity Hospital,	0033	06	08
Matheson's heirs, Broughton, .	0248	10	00
James Key, . .	0217	09	04
Alexander Key,	0078	00	00
Lochbank, . . .	0131	00	00
William Livingston's heirs.	0072	10	00
James Smith, Mutrishill,	0046	13	04
Robert Hill's heirs,	0014	10	00
Clockmiln, . .	0190	13	04
Earle of Roxburghe, .	0130	00	00
Graye's heirs, Drumdryen, . . .	0265	00	00
George Thompson's heirs, for Aikers, &c.,	0058	00	00
Turnbulls Aikers and houses, . .	0189	08	06
William Laurie, for high ridge at Westport,	0199	16	08

	£	s.	d.
William Lorimer at Potterrow,	0061	00	00
Saughtonhall,	1974	00	00
Damhead, .	0962	00	00
Dalrie Milnes,	0391	00	00
Patrick Broun's heirs, .	0200	00	00
Dean, Sir Patrick Nisbet,	1666	13	04
Hendrie, Dean, Younger,	0833	06	08
Westport, .	1041	08	00
King's Stables,	0290	07	00
Potterraw, ...	1292	08	00
James Duncan for his pairt of Lauristoun,	0164	00	00

APPENDIX B.

It would seem that, after the Revolution, Mr. Williamson and Sir Patrick Nisbet attempted to clear off old scores with Mushet. Apparently he was summarily dismissed from his office of 'Reider' at the church, and, on what grounds it is now impossible to discover, thrown into prison. The original books of the 'Gudeman of the Tolbooth,' at this time George Drummond, are still in existence, and from them the following entry is taken :—

'EDINBURGH, 29 *Septr.* 1690.

'Mr. John Mushet liberat by written consent, the tenor whereof follows : I, Mr. David Williamson, minister of the gospel at the West Kirk of Edinburgh, do hereby consent that Mr. John Mushet, prisoner in the Tolbooth of Edinburgh, at my instance, be presently set at liberty without any charge to be put at liberty against the Magistrates of Edinburgh. Declaring hereby, thir pr^{nts} shall be als effectual to the Magistrates and keeper of the Tolbooth of Edinburgh as if they were ane suspension and charge to put at libertie obtained at his instance against me.'

The same books should show the charge on which Mushet was imprisoned, but unfortunately, at some stage in their long existence, they have been but indifferently cared for ; many pages are wanting, while, owing to damp, the volume in which the charge against him should be found is practically destroyed and its contents lost. Mushet proved himself no contemptible antagonist. He raised an action against the West Kirk Session, presumably for wrongous dismissal and imprisonment. The matter is again and again mentioned in the records, but the notices, with the exception of the concluding one, throw very little light on the subject. By it, however, it would appear that Mushet had the best of the struggle, as the Kirk-Session then agreed to pay him the sum of 512 merks in order to stay further proceedings, and so the matter ended.

APPENDIX C.

FOUNTAINHALL records the fact that, in 1677, Sir Patrick Nisbet was formally accused, by Hepburn of Humbie, of perjury, and that his case was considered so desperate that his cousin, Sir John Nisbet, who was then Lord Advocate, advised him to give Hepburn 4000 merks in order to get a discharge of the process. Curious advice to come from a Lord Advocate ; but blood was thicker than water in those days ; and another cousin, Nisbet of Craigentinny, was willing to go even further than this. Through his instrumentality the principal papers in the case were borrowed from the Clerk of Court, and made away with ; and so Sir Patrick escaped further proceedings, though at the expense of his cousin, who suffered imprisonment for some time as a reward of his share in the exploit.